A YARN SHOP TO DIE FOR

A WONDERLAND BOOKS COZY MYSTERY
BOOK FIVE

M.P. BLACK

For my friends.

"The only way to have a friend is to be one."
— Ralph Waldo Emerson

CHAPTER 1

*T*he latest postcard looked innocent enough: on the front was a photo collage of tourist attractions in America, ranging from the Empire State Building to the iconic Paul Bunyan statue with his red checkered shirt and ax.

"That's the one in Bangor, Maine," Becca said, holding up the card for Alice and Ona to see. "Not the one in Portland, Oregon."

"It's not Paul Bunyan I'm worried about," Alice said.

Becca shrugged. "It's just some kook sending strange messages."

The three of them sat on the little benches against the bookshelves at Wonderland Books, drinking coffee from a thermos that Becca had brought from her diner. The bookstore was in a tiny house, a mere 400 square feet of space in a miniature log cabin crammed to the rafters with books. Ona —not only an innkeeper but also a master carpenter—had built the tiny house. Then Alice had turned it into her dream bookshop.

She treasured these moments, when she could sit with

her best friends and drink coffee and revel in the bookish coziness of her life. But this Friday morning, Becca had brought more than coffee. She'd brought a mystery: someone had been sending her poison-pen postcards.

While Becca poured everyone more coffee, Alice read the message on the back again, which, surprisingly, was type-written.

"'Hell is empty and all the devils are here.' It sounds like a quote."

Alice dug her phone out and searched online.

"I was right. It's from Shakespeare, from *The Tempest*."

"Like the rest," Ona said. She shuffled through the half a dozen other postcards Becca had received at the diner. She picked one at random and read it.

"'I never saw anybody take so long to dress, and with such little result.' Whoa, that's mean. I wish I knew who sent this. I'd have a thing or two to tell them…"

She lowered the card, her one visible eye pressed into a furious frown. A rhinestone-decorated eye-patch covered her other eye.

Hell hath no fury like an Ona scorned, Alice thought, and it brought a smile to her lips to think of how the three of them —Alice, Becca, and Ona—would stand up for each other. *Becca and Ona are my greatest defenders.*

She turned her attention back to the quote, which, she realized, sounded familiar.

"This is an Oscar Wilde quote," she said. "I'd bet money on it."

"It's from *The Importance of Being Earnest*," Becca confirmed, handing Alice a full cup of coffee. "I checked. In fact, after the first three or four, which I simply tossed in the trash, I did an online search. Each one is a literary quote."

"A quote that's meant to insult you," Ona said.

Becca shrugged. "Like I said, it's just some crazy person. Lorraine's also been receiving them. Beau, too."

Lorraine Maxwell ran the public library. Beau Bowers owned the Blithedale Theater.

"But I haven't," Ona said. "You, Alice?"

Alice shook her head.

Becca said, "Well, that's good. In any case, I thought you ladies might enjoy the mystery. Who could be sending these creative poison-pen postcards?"

Alice studied the front of each postcard, passing them, one by one, to Ona, who also looked closely at the pictures. There was nothing unusual about the postcards. They were the cheap touristy ones you could find in swivel racks across the country, appealing mostly to foreign tourists or the occasional cross-country road tripper. They featured photos of Niagara Falls, Mount Rushmore, and the Statue of Liberty.

Alice said, "They're too generic to tell us anything about the person. But I'm guessing that's intentional. The sender even used a typewriter—no doubt so we wouldn't recognize the handwriting."

There was a tap at the door. Alice handed the postcards to Becca again and shoved off the bench.

She opened the door.

Outside stood a blonde woman in a windbreaker, her shoulders dappled with raindrops from this morning's shower. Her hair, cut into a girlish bob, was held by a headband. Alice guessed she was in her mid-thirties.

She smiled, revealing a mouth crowded with oversized teeth.

"Is Becca here?"

Behind Alice, Becca said, "Oh, is that Trudy?"

Alice opened the door and, without more of an invitation, the woman stepped inside. She flung aside her wet windbreaker, letting it drop on the counter, and headed straight for Becca. Alice stared at the windbreaker for a moment before closing the front door. She tried not to feel annoyed that the woman would throw her wet jacket on the counter like that.

"I'm Trudy," the woman said, her voice as forceful as a goose's honk. "Hi!"

Alice and Ona introduced themselves.

"Trudy grew up in Blithedale," Becca explained. "She moved back recently to open a law firm."

"Lock, Stock, and Barrel," Trudy said.

"Beg your pardon?" Alice said.

"That's the name: Lock, Stock, and Barrel Law."

"Oh," Alice said. "Now that you mention it, I noticed a new office opening up..."

Trudy continued to smile. She stared at Alice, then Ona, then back at Alice, her intense blue eyes not blinking. All four of them were standing in a circle, staring at each other. It felt awkward. Should Alice say something?

"Uh, well, welcome back to Blithedale, Trudy."

"Alice also lived in Blithedale years ago and just came back," Becca said.

"Right," Trudy said. "Your mom died of cancer, so you moved away."

Alice's spine stiffened. The summary was accurate, but Trudy's directness hit hard—there was no effort to soften the mention of her mom's death.

"That's right...I came back because—"

"Because you bolted from the altar, ditching your fiancé." Trudy nodded. "I know. And then, after they tore down the wreck of a bookstore your mom used to own, you opened this tiny place."

Alice flinched at the words "wreck of a bookstore."

As if Mom had anything to do with Blithedale Books falling apart. That was Bunce's doing.

But Alice didn't challenge Trudy. She was getting the sense that Trudy lacked a social filter. Still, couldn't she be a little more polite?

A moment later, her theory about Trudy's lack of filter proved true when the woman referred to Ona's business, the Pemberley Inn, as "that rickety old Victorian" and to Ona as "the DIY lady who builds tiny houses nobody wants to buy."

Alice studied Ona's face. But whereas Ona had looked ready to bite someone's head off after reading the postcards Becca had received, she now looked relaxed, even amused.

"Yup," she said. "That's me."

"Becca," Trudy said, turning her high-beam eyes onto Becca. "You wanted to talk to me?"

Becca nodded. "I was wondering whether you'd thought more about the knitting club. I'd love to join you."

"Hey, it's a free country. I'm going. You can join if you want. Speaking of which,"—Trudy checked her wristwatch—"I can't waste more time hanging around here. I have work to do."

Alice bristled. *Waste time? You think the rest of us don't have work, too?*

Ona must've sensed her reaction, because she slipped an arm around her shoulders and gave her a little reassuring squeeze. Leaning close, she said, "Let it go."

Trudy grabbed her jacket from the counter and with a holler—"bye!"—that would've made a football coach proud, she swept out of Wonderland Books.

Alice let out a long breath. "Wow, intense."

"She's—" Becca paused. "—special."

"And yet you're joining a knitting club with her. You're a good person, Becca Frye."

"I feel sorry for her. I remember what she was like when she was a kid: Awkward. Excluded by other kids. She had one friend, and when that friend left Blithedale, Trudy was all alone. While the other kids roamed the woods or met at each other's homes, she used to hang out at the diner or the public library, reading magazines or books. I felt bad for her. But I didn't do anything to help." She sighed. "I wish I had. I guess now's my chance to set things right."

Alice beckoned for Becca to come closer so she could put an arm around her. The three of them stood together. Ona said, "Alice is right, Becca. You're a good person."

"You would do the same," Becca said.

Ona laughed. "Join a knitting club to make Trudy feel welcome? Oh, I'm not so sure…"

Becca looked down at her feet. It wasn't like her to look so uncomfortable—as if she were concealing something embarrassing.

"Becca?" Alice said. "What are you not telling us?"

"Well, the thing is, I was hoping you'd help out."

"Help out with…?"

Becca looked up and smiled apologetically.

"Oh, no." Ona backed away. "You don't mean join the knitting club?"

"It's just once a week," Becca said. "At the Yarn Shoppe. It so happens that Edna's starting up her knitting club again. It'll be great. We'll knit and talk and drink tea…"

"Talking and drinking tea I can do. But knitting? *No, gracias.*" Ona shook her head emphatically. "Sorry, Becca. I can't sign up for that."

Color rose to Becca's face.

"Becca," Alice said, taking one of Becca's hands. "Out with it."

"I already signed us up."

"Us?" Ona gasped. "Me, too?"

Becca nodded.

"We start knitting on Sunday night."

Ona groaned.

CHAPTER 2

*A*t its far end, Main Street forked, sending cars off to Tilbury Town or deeper into the Blithedale Woods. About 20 feet from the crumbling curb stood the Yarn Shoppe. Trees craned over its roof, creating a natural awning that threw the store into shadow, especially this late in the day.

Alice had never noticed the shop before for a simple reason: it was half hidden in the woods. Mother Nature had been tough on the little store. A thick layer of lichen covered the roof. Brambly bushes crowded around the building. And on one wall, a large stain suggested there was serious water damage.

"Seen better days," Ona said.

Alice eyed it dubiously. "It is still in business, isn't it?"

"Edna must get some customers. People pass the shop whenever they hike the North Trail."

A hiking trail running past the Yarn Shoppe and into the gloom of the dense Blithedale Woods looked well worn. Obviously, there was still foot traffic down at this end of

Main Street. But how many people actually came to visit the Yarn Shoppe?

This was the first time Alice herself was visiting the small store. It had been many years since she'd done any knitting—in fact, more than 20 years—and until now she hadn't considered picking up the hobby again.

"Maybe it'll turn out to be a blast," she told Ona as they walked into the cooler air under the trees.

Ona snorted. "I doubt it."

"Why're you so against knitting?"

"It's not an ideological thing, if that's what you think. It's that—well, I'm not—I just—" Ona ran a hand across her neck. She let out a quick breath. "All right. The truth? I'm bad at it."

"That's all? Well, I'm bad at it, too."

"No, no. I mean, I'm *bad*. Terrible. Atrocious. An embarrassment to knitters worldwide."

Alice laughed. "I don't believe it. The woman who can install new electrical outlets and fix leaks in the roof at the Pemberley Inn, the woman who builds her own tiny houses, the woman who—"

"The woman who had to go to the emergency room after injuring herself on a knitting needle. True story."

"You're exaggerating."

"Am I? I'll show you my scars later."

Alice, laughing, pulled open the door. A little brass bell dinged once overhead. On the hardwood floor stood baskets overflowing with balls of yarn in all the colors of the rainbow. Even more yarn filled the shelves along the walls. Stands held knitting needles. A metal rack displayed books and magazines on knitting and crocheting, though the paperbacks had yellowed with age and the people on the magazine covers sported hairstyles from decades ago.

The comforting smell of yarn filled the space—like a

childhood memory of a wool blanket—but also something else underneath that: a mustiness that made her wrinkle her nose.

A woman emerged from a back room, closing the door behind her, and smiling as she saw Alice and Ona.

"Hello, I'm Edna," she said. "We spoke on the phone and —" She stopped herself. "But, silly me, you're not from the security company, are you?"

Alice guessed Edna was in her seventies. She had short, gray hair that coiled into curls at her ears and a ruddy face that made her look as if she'd just stepped inside from a winter storm. Her stubby nose was the color of a fresh strawberry, only a shade lighter than her red knitted cardigan.

"You were expecting someone from a security company?"

"Just a little break-in. Nothing stolen. But it's finally convinced me I need one of those newfangled alarm thingamajigs."

Alice considered how many decades home and business alarm systems had been available. In terms of technology, Edna might be a little behind the times.

"Anyway," she said with a smile. "What can I do for you, young ladies?"

"We're here about the knitting club."

The woman put her hands together, her warm smile growing even warmer. "Oh, wonderful. Just wonderful. More people joining. You can sign up here."

She showed them a sign-up sheet on a clipboard dangling from a string on a hook.

"We're actually already signed up," Alice said, pointing to the list.

"Delightful," the woman said.

Yes, there she was on the list: "Alice Hartford." And above her name, it said, "Becca Frye." Below her own name, Becca had also written "Ona Rodriguez." Alice scanned the list for other names she might recognize. There was Trudy: "Trudy Lockstock." So her law firm's clever title at least had some connection to her own name. Below her name was another Alice recognized, "Beau Bowers."

"I didn't know Beau knitted," she said.

"Oh, he's rather new to knitting," Edna said.

"Jolene Burr," Alice read, pointing out the next name. It was the only other one on the list so far. She didn't know any Jolenes or Burrs.

Edna's eyebrows touched in a frown. "Jolene's an experienced knitter. Frankly, I don't even know why she's bothering to come…"

A sharp note had crept into Edna's voice, which made Alice look at her. But Edna seemed to shake the frown off and then questioned them about their needs.

With a friendly smile, she assured them they needn't be nervous about the knitting club. "I'm calling it a 'club' this time. But I've run these things many times before. Often, I call them knitting circles, and that's all it is: a group of women—oh, and this time a man, too—sitting in a circle, knitting. We help each other, enjoy some tea or coffee and cookies, talk."

"You make it sound harmless," Ona said, apparently still unconvinced.

"Completely harmless," Edna said. "No one gets hurt. Unless you get really badly tangled in your yarn," she added with a chuckle. "Now, let's look at what tools and yarn you need…"

They spent the next 15 minutes looking at knitting needles, yarn, and books with patterns. Coming in, Alice had imagined she'd buy a pair of knitting needles and a couple of balls of yarn. Little did she realize she'd underestimated the accessories she might need—at least according to Edna.

Soon, Alice was holding two kinds of knitting needles (one pair made of metal, the other of wood), five balls of yarn (three acrylic, two wool), a pair of embroidery scissors, a knitting gauge, stitch markers, and a packet of stitch holders.

"Er…am I really going to use all this?" she asked Edna.

"If you're serious about your knitting, yes."

"I'm just trying it out. It's been twenty-some years…"

"All the more reason to have the right tools. You don't want to get discouraged because you don't have the right tools."

While Alice was considering this bit of commercial wisdom—or upsell—the little bell dinged again to announce another customer. Edna glanced over and the warm smile snuffed out, like a candle flame, replaced by a cold, thin line.

A striking woman—also in her seventies, Alice guessed—strode into the store, her high heels clacking on the hardwood floor. With her sculpted nose in the air, she looked around. As she turned to the side, the skin on her neck stretched on one side.

Plastic surgery, Alice thought. *And plenty of it.*

The woman's lips formed a perennial pout, half, perhaps, the effect of artificial filler, the other half her attitude.

"Still hiding in your little ruin in the woods, Edna? I'm surprised you haven't turned into a mushroom by now." She picked up a ball of yarn and then dropped it, as if she worried about how hygienic it might be. She made a show of wiping her hands on her skirt. "Ah, there it is."

The woman strode over to the clipboard. But instead of reaching for the pen that dangled from a string next to it, she dug into her Louis Vuitton bag and extracted a fountain pen. She wrote her name on the list.

"There," she said, as she finished with a flourish. As she put her pen away, she looked down her sharp nose at Edna. "I'll see you on Sunday. It'll be just like old times, won't it?"

Edna's voice was low, almost a whisper. "What do you want, Lillian?"

The other woman, Lillian, smiled. Her perfectly even teeth flashed. "What do you think I want? I want to enjoy an evening with my oldest friends. I heard Jolene's coming, so why shouldn't I? We'll do some knitting, sip your store-brand tea, and reminisce about the good old days." She took a step toward Edna and narrowed her eyes. "Remember those, Edna? The good old days?"

Edna said nothing.

Lillian stared at her for a moment longer. Then she broke away and strode out, slamming the door behind her.

Alice realized she was clutching her yarn and knitting tools to her chest, clasping everything with such force that the knitting needles were jabbing her.

"What," she whispered to Ona, "was that?"

Ona shook her head. "Something tells me this knitting club won't be as cozy as advertised."

CHAPTER 3

*A*lice and Ona made an agreement: each of them would practice their knitting during the workday on Saturday, and then they'd meet after hours to share notes.

In between helping customers find the books they wanted, Alice worked on a potholder. Who would use the potholder? She didn't know. That wasn't the point. The point was she'd picked one of the easiest patterns.

The knitting sparked interest and made people more talkative than usual. Alice wondered whether knitting, like owning a dog or having a baby, was the real trick to winning friends and influencing people.

In the afternoon, Mr. and Mrs. Oriel, a retired couple who had recently retired to live in Blithedale, came to the store to buy another stack of mystery novels. They gushed about her new hobby.

"We used to knit," Mrs. Oriel said.

"Both of us," Mr. Oriel said.

"We'd make little hats or gloves for our grandchildren."

"Or scarves. I made a scarf for you one year, didn't I, dear?"

"Oh, yes…that beautiful purple scarf."

They beamed at each other and interlaced their fingers. Alice liked how often they held hands. They seemed inseparable. They even wore identical clothes and glasses, giving them the air of having been cast from the same mold.

"We don't knit anymore, though," Mrs. Oriel said.

"Quilting's our passion now," Mr. Oriel said.

"Yes, quilting is very much our passion."

That word—"passion"—seemed to spark something between them. They eyed each other like a pair of teenagers and Alice suddenly felt superfluous.

After wishing Alice the best of luck with her knitting, they left. They were the last customers of the day. She tidied up, locked away the cash, and then grabbed her knitting before heading out.

A spring breeze met her outside, tugging at her like a happy puppy. It made her smile. After the bare, skeletal trees of winter, it was a relief to see green leaves on the trees again. Birds were singing. The rich forest floor humus mixed with the first scents of springtime flowers.

Alice had promised to drop off a book at Andrea's cafe, Bonsai & Pie, at the other end of Main Street. With that done, she turned around and headed back toward the Pemberley Inn, her home.

The route took her past the new law office. A man on a ladder was hoisting up a sign that said, "Lock, Stock, and Barrel Law."

She stopped and watched the man use a power drill to bolt the sign to the wall.

A name like that was refreshing, she supposed, after the usual dry, humorless law firm names. But it made you wonder how serious the lawyer was. Law firms were like banks. You wanted them to be boring, didn't you?

But Trudy might not be a good judge of that. If she had

no sense of social decorum, maybe she also didn't have a strong sense of what tone to adopt when naming her business.

With her mind on Trudy, Alice turned to continue on her way to the inn, and noticed a woman across the street. She wore a hoodie with the hood up, plus a pair of large sunglasses. She was also looking at the law firm.

For a moment, she took off the sunglasses and rubbed them against the fabric on her hoodie, cleaning the lenses. In that instant, a spark of recognition flared in Alice's mind.

Wait a minute, I know you...

The woman, around 30 years old, like Alice herself, slipped the sunglasses back on and turned on her heels. She hurried down the street.

Yes, we've met. But who are you?

Alice couldn't think of an answer to her question. It felt like déjà vu—that strange feeling of experiencing something for the second time. So, where and when had she met this woman before?

It would come to her eventually, she decided, and turned her nose toward the Pemberley Inn.

The Pemberley Inn, named after Mr. Darcy's estate in Jane Austen's *Pride and Prejudice*, was an old Victorian mansion that Ona had converted into Blithedale's only hotel. When Alice had first come to town, Ona had offered her a free room. These days, Alice paid long-term rent, an arrangement that made both her and Ona happy.

Ona was waiting for her in the lounge, sitting on a couch and struggling with a pair of knitting needles. She frowned at them as they clacked together. And slipped. She growled and threw down the knitting.

"Enough." She looked up at Alice. "How about we go out back and saw something? Or hammer it?"

Alice laughed. "Oh, no, you don't. We have to get ready

for tomorrow's knitting club. If nothing else, we have to look competent so we can keep an eye on the drama."

"It's going to be a soap opera, isn't it?"

Alice plopped down on the couch next to Ona.

"Who is this Lillian woman, anyway?"

"Lillian McGlinty. She lives in a mansion in the 'fancy' part of town. Her husband was rich. Can't remember his name. Phil or Will or Bill."

"Was? Past tense?"

"She's been a widow for a few years, yeah."

"And what's her gripe with Edna?"

Ona shook her head. "No idea. But I'm guessing we'll find out tomorrow night."

They settled down to knitting. Alice was surprised to see that Ona hadn't been kidding: she really couldn't knit. She tried. But it was as if her hands were three times too big and her fingers simply wouldn't make the smooth turns required.

Alice was just as surprised to discover that her own abilities were far better than she'd assumed. Her mom had taught her to knit when she was a kid—she must've been 7 years old the first time she held a pair of knitting needles, a couple years before her mom's cancer diagnosis—and she found the lessons had stuck. It was like picking up where she'd left off, and soon she settled into a pleasant flow as she threaded, looped, and pulled the yarn.

After working on their knitting for another 30 minutes, Ona put down her needles and yarn.

"All right," she said. "I've been patient. Can we go play now, please?"

Alice laughed. "Yes, let's go play."

Ona jumped up and headed for the doors that led to the porch out back. She pushed them open, letting in the cool spring breeze.

"Ah," Ona said, appreciating the view. "This is more like it."

"You do love your building."

"You have your sleuthing. I have my building."

Ona went down the porch stairs and Alice followed. Behind the Pemberley Inn was a small village of tiny houses. There were mini Swiss-style chalets, one built to look like a Western saloon, and a yellow house with pink shutters that was clearly inspired by Villa Villekulla, Pippi Longstocking's house—only it was a fraction of the size.

Ona had built each tiny house herself. She constructed more than she could sell, in part because Mayor MacDonald wouldn't change the building code in town to allow smaller homes and businesses, and in part because Ona loved to build.

At the center of the little village was Ona's showroom, a tiny house decorated with furniture to show buyers what they'd be getting, as well as an outdoor workspace with a workbench and a weatherproof case for tools.

Ona got out a hammer, saw, and drill.

As they got started on the carpentry together, Alice's mind drifted off to the woman in the hoodie she'd seen on Main Street. She tried to fit the face into different places—the bookstore, the diner, even her old life in the city—but she couldn't remember spending time with her at Wonderland Books or any of the other places.

So how could the woman look so familiar?

The little mystery kept her mind busy as she helped Ona saw planks for another house.

CHAPTER 4

*A*s usual on a Sunday morning, Alice went to the bookstore. But she didn't open for business. Instead, entering her tiny house cabin, she left the sign saying, "Sorry, We're Closed," and closed the door behind her.

She stood inside, listening. All was quiet. And yet she sensed a kind of hum, a gentle vibration of books, the inexplicable aura that made bookstores and libraries so welcoming. It was a feeling she would forever associate with her mom.

Today was the anniversary of her mom's passing, and she wanted to mark the day. She spread an old quilt out on the floor—the kind her mom would've loved—and placed a candle on a wooden board in the middle. She sat down on the quilt. She lit the candle. Then she opened a copy of *Alice's Adventures in Wonderland*, the one, in fact, she'd recovered from her mom's old bookstore after it was demolished.

She found the part where her namesake was playing croquet with the Queen of Hearts, a passage that she remembered fondly, because she and her mom had laughed about the flamingo. She read:

"The chief difficulty Alice found at first was in managing her flamingo: she succeeded in getting its body tucked away, comfortably enough, under her arm, with its legs hanging down, but generally, just as she had got its neck nicely straightened out, and was going to give the hedgehog a blow with its head, it would twist itself round and look up in her face, with such a puzzled expression that she could not help bursting out laughing: and when she had got its head down, and was going to begin again, it was very provoking to find that the hedgehog had unrolled itself, and was in the act of crawling away: besides all this, there was generally a ridge or furrow in the way wherever she wanted to send the hedgehog to, and, as the doubled-up soldiers were always getting up and walking off to other parts of the ground, Alice soon came to the conclusion that it was a very difficult game indeed."

Alice smiled to herself.

"I loved reading this with you," she whispered to the bookstore. "I still do."

She knew there was no such thing as ghosts, but somehow she still felt her mom's presence among the books.

She would perform this little ritual every year from now on. There was no grave she could visit: after the cremation, her mom's ashes were scattered across a beach. Lighting a candle and reading aloud, sharing this kind of joyful intimacy again, was the closest she could come to communing with her mom.

She felt close now. But that hadn't always been the case.

For years, Alice felt that the memory of her mom was dispersing as easily as dandelion seeds in the wind, leaving only an empty stalk behind. It was a sad little thing for a girl to hold on to, barely a memory at all.

But once she'd come back to Blithedale, she'd sensed her

mom. It was as if particles of her mom continued to float in the air. By the time she opened Wonderland Books, some remnant of her mom gathered and took shape, blossoming into fuller memories. This ritual was a way to catch more of those floating memories.

Alice put down the book. Again, she listened to the store. She thought about her mom and what she would've thought about her daughter coming back to Blithedale, opening Wonderland Books, and getting involved in all these mysteries.

"You would've liked that," she said, "wouldn't you?"

After all, Alice's mom had been passionate about books and bookselling—plus, she'd done some sleuthing of her own.

"Like mother, like daughter," Alice said and smiled.

Then she picked up the book again and continued to read to her mom.

CHAPTER 5

"What's our code word?" Ona whispered.

Alice raised an eyebrow. "Code word?"

"Yeah, like I say 'pumpernickel' or 'Montreal' and then you know it's time to make an excuse and leave."

"Ona, it's going to be fine."

Ona looked around her, casting a dubious eye on the Yarn Shoppe's interior.

"So you say…"

Edna had arranged chairs in a perfect circle, so the knitters could face each other. One of the wooden chairs had arm rests. On the seat lay a pair of knitting needles and a ball of yarn. This was clearly Edna's own chair.

A low table in the middle accommodated a carafe of water, glasses, thermoses with tea and coffee, and cups. Edna bustled into the main space from the back room with a plate of cookies and put it down.

"I am so thrilled you're here," she said, her cheeks bright red and her eyes sparkling. "So thrilled. Now, come, come, sit down."

Ona lowered herself onto a chair. Alice sat on her left.

"Tea? Coffee?"

Alice and Ona both chose decaf coffee, and Edna poured them a cup each. The coffee tasted of wet ashes.

"Do you have any milk?" Ona asked.

"Oh," Edna said. "I forgot the creamer."

She hurried out back and came back with a container of powdered coffee creamer and a spoon. Alice and Ona heaped the powder into the coffee. Now it tasted like syrupy ashes.

Alice poured herself a glass of water. Ona reached for a cookie.

Alice, who was used to the generous spreads Ona put out for guests at the Pemberley Inn, sometimes with a dozen varieties of doughnuts, thought the refreshments left a little to be desired, but she reminded herself that this was about the knitting, not the coffee and baked goods. Even if the fee for joining the knitting club was high enough to warrant something tastier…

"So, ladies," Edna said, rubbing her hands together, "tell me all about your knitting."

Ona shrank into her seat, suddenly 100 percent focused on nibbling her cookie. Alice covered for her, telling Edna about how she'd remembered some of her mom's lessons from years ago.

"It all came back to me," she said, "and now it's going pretty well."

"I remember your mother, of course," Edna said.

Alice smiled. "And her old bookstore."

"Naturally. She ran a wonderful bookstore. But your mother also helped me once."

"Helped you?"

"She solved a problem. An awful problem." Edna's face grew serious. Then shook herself, like shaking off a chill. "But let's not talk about that tonight. We're here to get cozy, do some knitting, and get to know each other better."

At that moment, the front door opened, and two women stepped inside.

One of them said, "We already know each other far too well."

It was Lillian. Behind her came a woman who, apart from being a similar age, seemed the exact opposite of Lillian: where Lillian stood tall on her high heels, this woman, in threadbare flats, was short; where Lillian wore a designer blazer and silk shirt, this woman wore a drab knitted sweater that had lost its color with many washes; and where Lillian stood straight, looking down her nose at the gathering, this woman cowered in the doorway, reminding Alice of a timid rabbit.

"Welcome, Lillian," Edna said, all the honeyed sweetness gone from her voice. Then she turned to the other woman and her voice turned even chillier as she said, "And you."

"The best friends reunited," Lillian said and let out a single, harsh laugh.

Ona nudged Alice. She whispered, "Best friends? Wonder what worst enemies looks like."

Alice waved at the newcomers. "Hi, I'm Alice."

Lillian smiled, not showing her teeth. "Lillian McGlinty."

The timid woman took a step forward. In her hands, she clutched a bag with knitting needles sticking out at one end. She said, "Jolene—" She looked anxiously at Lillian and then at Edna, took a quick, shallow breath as if to gather courage, and added, "—Burr."

"Sit," Edna snapped. She turned on her heels and padded out into the back room. Alice had the feeling that she'd left, not because she needed to get supplies, but that she couldn't stand to face the two newcomers, Lillian and Jolene.

Lillian looked at the chairs, spotted the one Alice guessed was Edna's, and with a smirk, chose a seat to the right of that one.

Jolene stood for a moment, wide-eyed, staring at the chairs. She moved toward one, then stopped, moved in the opposite direction.

"Oh, for God's sake," Lillian said. "Stop being so pathetic, Jolene, and sit your butt down."

Jolene's face blanched, and she mumbled something, then made a decision and slipped onto the empty seat on the other side of Edna's.

The four of them—Alice, Ona, Lillian, and Jolene—sat in awkward silence. Ona nibbled her cookie.

Luckily, the tense atmosphere was broken by others arriving.

First, Beau came, giving Alice and Ona hugs, and telling them all about the latest bands playing at the Blithedale Theater. He gushed about a touring theater troupe and a comedy act he'd booked.

"We've got so many amazing artists lined up for the year."

Alice and Ona had already seen the program, but it was a relief to have the Yarn Shoppe filled with his enthusiasm, so Alice encouraged him to talk.

"So, what brings you to the knitting club?" Beau asked.

"It was Becca's idea," Alice said, leaving it at that.

"Excellent idea. I've been looking for a hobby that's relaxing. That's why I'm here." He heaved a heavy sigh. "This theater business is stressful. There are so many moving parts, and you never know if a show will be a success or a huge drain on finances."

Beau had taken over the theater after his sister's death and transformed the old movie theater into a thriving venue for music, dance, theater, comedy, and other performing arts. But Alice could see the toll it was taking on him.

She put a hand on his arm. "Then it's a good thing you've taken up knitting."

While Beau told Alice about his efforts to learn to knit, Becca and Trudy arrived.

"Everyone's already here," Becca said and smiled.

"Well, this is barebones," Trudy said, gesturing toward the refreshments. "Guess it's all about the knitting, huh? Or about making a bigger profit margin."

Alice flinched at the unfiltered comment. It was what she herself had been thinking, but Trudy was clearly one of those people who simply couldn't stop a thought from reaching their lips.

Trudy continued: "I remember when this place was a thriving business, but the store sure has seen better days. That's not surprising. It's in a terrible location. Plus, the whole place feels so yesteryear."

"Quaint and cozy," Becca said gently, offering a positive spin.

Trudy shrugged. She held up a little bag with knitting needles and yarn. "I've got my tools. So when do we start?"

Edna emerged from the back room, her warm smile back on her face.

"Everyone who signed up is here, so please, take a seat and we'll get started."

Trudy sat down next to Jolene. Becca sat next to Trudy, with Ona on her other side.

Edna went around her chair and opened a window right behind it, leaving it slightly ajar. Alice was glad she did: between the smell of bad coffee and that mustiness she'd noticed earlier, the shop was getting stuffy.

Edna turned around and hesitated. She'd apparently seen who sat on either side of her: Lillian to her right and Jolene to her left.

Lillian smirked at her, her tight skin tightening even more across her onionskin face. Jolene smiled, but with her eyes downcast, the smile soon died a timid death.

Once seated, Edna said, "Thank you all for coming. For decades, I've run Blithedale's knitting circles—or clubs, or whatever you want to call them—and it's been many years now since I hosted the last one. But this one, if all goes well," —for an instant, Alice noticed, Edna glanced left and then right, apparently unable to keep herself from looking at Lillian and Jolene—"won't be the last. So, let's get started."

On the word "started," the door opened. Alice turned to see who came in, as did everyone else.

In the doorway stood a tall, gaunt woman. Like Edna, Lillian, and Jolene, she must be in her seventies. A sensible ponytail pinned her gray hair back. Her face was free of makeup. Her clothes suggested woodsy living: a long gray skirt, a red flannel buttoned up to the throat, and a hunter's vest over that. A big wooden crucifix hanging from a chain around her throat was her only jewelry.

She said, "'Behold, I stand at the door, and knock: if any man hear my voice, and open the door, I will come in to him.'"

"Hildegarde," Edna said. "What a pleasant surprise. You're not on our sign-up list."

Lillian muttered, "'Pleasant' isn't the word I would've chosen…"

Hildegarde, whose hearing was clearly sharp, stared at Lillian with the frowning disapproval of a fire-and-brimstone preacher. She shut the door behind her.

"Let me get you a chair," Edna said.

"I can get a chair," Hildegarde said. "'For God hath not given us the spirit of fear; but of power, and of love, and of a sound mind.'"

"Good grief," Lillian said, this time not bothering to keep her voice down. "There's a Bible quote for everything, isn't there?"

Hildegarde grabbed a chair near the back of the store and

returned with it. She stood towering over Lillian, looking down at her. Lillian gazed up at Hildegarde, giving her an icy stare. She said, "You can find another spot, Hildie. I'm comfortable here."

Hildegarde waited. But Lillian seemed to feel she had all the time in the world. She ignored Hildegarde, picked up her knitting, and worked the needles with smooth expertise.

A small voice from across the circle said, "Hildegarde, I can make room…"

Jolene had made the offer. She inched her chair toward Edna's, making a tiny space between herself and Trudy. But Hildegarde set down her chair by Edna's side, making it clear that she wanted Jolene to shift her seat the other way.

Everyone in the circle—everyone but Lillian—pushed their chairs back to widen the circle and make room, the chair legs scraping and screeching against the hardwood floor. Jolene shifted her chair. Hildegarde inserted herself between Edna and Jolene.

The interruption didn't last long, but it shifted the mood yet again. The volume of conversation dropped. Alice kept stealing glances at Hildegarde, wondering if she was being watched. Hildegarde reminded her of a strict chaperone, whose disapproving stare swept the circle, studying each one of them and judging them.

But Edna seemed unfazed by Hildegarde's arrival. She launched into an explanation of the principles of knitting. She sprinkled her talk with rhymes and puns: "Practicing for hours can make anyone a little loopy…but knitters aren't quitters…even when we feel we're at our knits end…"

Alice found Edna's advice and demonstrations of technique not only impressive but also helpful. Obviously, she'd done this many times before.

But there was one moment when her friendly, patient pedagogy imploded.

Edna had showed the circle how to start off with a simple twisted loop instead of a slipknot to avoid having the knot be visible when you're knitting in the round. Jolene was trying it out and showed Edna her work with a bashful, "Like this, Edna?"

Edna snapped at her: "Don't be a show-off, Jolene."

Jolene flinched, withdrew her knitting, as if a snake had lunged at her, and she hunched over her work.

What had gotten into Edna? She seemed so sweet most of the time, but whenever she engaged with Lillian and, even more so, Jolene, the sweetness turned sour.

Hildegarde knitted, too. But despite sitting among everyone else, it continued to seem as if she sat outside the circle, looking in.

It fell on Alice, Beau, Becca, and Trudy to maintain the good cheer. But Trudy wasn't much help. After the incident between Edna and Jolene, she said, "Why do you ladies hang out if you don't even like each other?"

Edna said, "The circle is open to anyone who wants to come, my dear." She smiled at Trudy. "Even if some of our guests aren't people we'd want to invite into our homes."

Trudy shrugged. "You could always tell them not to come next time. It's your circle. Or say what you really think. Stop beating around the bush."

Edna's smiled didn't falter, though it looked like the fixed smile of a wax doll. She said, "It's a helpful suggestion, Trudy. I'll consider it."

"Meanwhile," Becca said, "we're here to have fun, aren't we?"

Beau nodded vigorously. His expression had turned more and more pinched with worry as the tension grew among the women. He'd been making more mistakes, dropping stitches and, distracted by the drama, putting down his knitting and forgetting which direction he'd been going.

"Are you all right?" Alice whispered.

"Maybe this was a mistake," Beau said. "Maybe I should've signed up for yoga instead. I can only imagine it's much less stressful." He took a deep breath and let out a sigh. "Guess I expected Winnie-the-Pooh coziness, not a rehash of *Who's Afraid of Virginia Woolf?*"

He was right. What should've been a cozy evening, where the most stressful thing that could happen was dropping a stitch, had turned out to be tense and unpleasant. Alice considered checking the time. Out of the corner of her eye, she noticed Ona looking at her wristwatch.

Ona caught her glance. "Another hour to go."

"We can do it."

Ona nodded. "For Becca, anything."

Becca and Trudy huddled together, comparing stitches. At least Becca's purpose seemed to be fulfilled.

I hope Trudy feels welcome, Alice thought. *Though her directness doesn't do her any favors.*

In a whisper, Alice agreed with Ona, "For Becca, anything."

"Besides," Ona muttered, "it can't get any worse, can it?"

At that moment, the lights cut out. The room plunged into darkness.

CHAPTER 6

*I*n the dark, Alice froze.

"Alice?" Ona said.

"Right here."

"Me too," Becca said.

The sound of chairs creaking. One of them scraping. A clatter, maybe a pair of knitting pins dropping to the floor. Someone let out an oomph, and there was a thud and the glasses on the table rattled.

Then Jolene crying out: "I can't see, I can't see—oh, God."

"Jesus Christ," Lillian added, "will someone turn on the lights?"

Hildegarde's stern voice cut through the darkness: "'You shall not misuse the name of the Lord your God, for the Lord will not hold anyone guiltless who misuses his name.'"

"Aw, cut it out, Hildegarde," Lillian snapped. "Jolene's terrified of the dark."

"'Even though I walk through the darkest valley,'" Hildegarde said, more gently now, and apparently directly to Jolene, "'I will fear no evil, for you are with me.'"

Alice dug her phone out of her pocket and found the flashlight function.

A beam of light shot out of her phone. It caught Hildegarde's face, which was as impassive and impressive as a stone carving. She didn't even blink.

Alice swept the light across the circle. Jolene had pulled herself up into as small a ball as she could—her legs tucked under her on the chair, her arms wrapped around her knees, and her head down. She was trembling. Once again, it made Alice think of a rabbit.

Her beam swept across Trudy, who said, "Bet it's faulty wiring." Becca lit up, followed by Ona, and then Alice turned to her other side, casting light on Beau, who looked deathly pale. Lillian, next, threw one hand up to shield her eyes from the glare of the flashlight.

She said, "Edna, really, what's with the light show?"

But by then Alice's flashlight had reached Edna's chair. It was empty. For a moment, Alice assumed their host had left her seat to deal with the power outage, but the light caught a shape on the floor, and Alice got to her feet so she could crane over the low table and illuminate whatever was lying there.

Not whatever. Whoever.

It was Edna. She'd fallen forward in the chair and collapsed on the floor. Alice thought of the oomph she'd heard. Edna, with those bright cheeks, might've had a heart attack. She dismissed the idea. Because the light caught an object sticking out of Edna's back.

My God, is that a...?

Ona was on her feet, too, standing by Alice's side. She put words to Alice's thoughts when she said, "A knitting needle."

Behind them, Beau or Becca or Trudy lit the flashlight on their phone, brightening the room.

Lillian must've seen Edna then, because she drew in a sharp breath.

Hildegarde was closest to Edna and crouched down, putting a hand on the woman's neck. Alice and Ona rounded the table, and both crouched down by Edna. Hildegarde shook her head.

"No pulse," she said.

"I'll call Chief Jimbo," Beau said.

"Chief Jimbo resigned, remember?" Becca said. "He's in Florida visiting his dad. Call the state police instead."

"Or is it the county sheriff we should call?" Beau wondered.

"Stop arguing," Trudy said, "and call 9-1-1."

"Trudy's right," Ona said. "Someone stabbed Edna. We should call the cops and—"

A faint sound caught Alice's attention and made her look up. The window behind Edna's chair stood open. In the darkness outside, a shadow moved, a shape shifting in the blackness. Someone stood outside, peering in.

"Hey," Alice called out.

But by the time she'd swept her flashlight upward to see who it was, a rustle sounded in the thicket outside and the person vanished.

Alice didn't hesitate. She jumped up and leaped toward the front door, striking the table with her leg—pain flaring, something clattering—and then she flung open the front door and rushed outside. She swung left and right. Night had swallowed the woods, leaving only dark-gray columns amidst a deeper darkness. But there—she aimed her flashlight at what she saw—there ran a shadow, flitting through the trees.

Alice sprinted after the shadowy figure.

"Hey!" she cried out again.

The beam from her phone bobbed and shook, a wild light

dancing across the giant trees. It made the woods come alive. Branches seemed to sweep upward in fright, horrified by the glare. Tree trunks crept back. Others loomed taller, attempting to frighten her, and half succeeding.

She lost the shadow. Then her light grazed it again to the far right, and she changed direction. Was she gaining on her quarry? Maybe. You couldn't tell how far it was in the dark. But she thought so. She hoped so. She—

Something clamped down hard on her foot and she cried out in pain and fell forward. The ground slammed against her knees and stomach, and then her chin. A sharp object—a stick—dug into her neck. The nightmare smell of wet dirt filled her nostrils, and she gulped for air.

She swatted away the stick. She rolled around on her side, the pain from falling already throbbing in her chest and arms. The pain in her knees and foot was sharper.

She'd held on to her phone, thank goodness, and she threw light on what had snagged her: a giant root. It had tripped her, and she'd been unlucky enough to hit an old, rotten log with her knees.

But lucky not to hit a rock with my chin, she told herself. *Or my skull.*

She staggered to her feet, the waves of pain crashing over her. But she raised her light and swept the beam across the trees to find the figure she was chasing.

The mammoth columns of trees stretched into the dark. But otherwise the Blithedale Woods were silent. Her flashlight caught no movement in the forest.

For a while, she stood still, wondering if she'd suddenly see a figure emerge from hiding or hear a distant sound. But the woods were quiet. All was still.

Finally, she admitted it to herself: the shadow was gone.

CHAPTER 7

" $\mathcal{L}$ adies."

Captain Burlap, the state police criminal investigator, took off his cap and eased himself onto the leatherette seat in the booth. Alice, Becca, and Ona had been expecting him. After he arrived to the crime scene with the EMT crew and the county coroner, he'd asked Alice and her friends to meet him at the What the Dickens Diner in a couple of hours, so they could talk.

He glanced up at the framed print of an illustration from one of Charles Dickens' serialized novels. This one was from David Copperfield. The scene was of a man lying in his canopy bed, apparently sick, but with one arm draped over a treasure chest. The caption said, "I find Mr. Barkis 'going out with the Tide.'"

"I don't remember that from David Copperfield," Burlap said. "But then it's been a long time since I read the novel. Maybe it's time I reread it in my spare time. I just have to find some spare time…" He ran a hand over his stubbly chin and chuckled. "The problem is that I seem to have mislaid all my spare time. And a murder in Blithedale won't help me find it."

He turned his attention to Alice, Becca, and Ona. He dug out a notebook from a pocket, flipped it open, and got out a pen.

"All right, why don't you tell me what happened, step by step, starting with why you joined the victim's knitting club tonight?"

Becca explained her plans to make Trudy feel more welcome, and how she'd suggested that she and Trudy could join a social club.

"A knitting club, in particular?" Burlap asked. "Did you suggest the victim's knitting club?"

"Well, I'm not sure. I think I did. Or I suggested a book club and then Trudy said she didn't have time for a book club, not with how busy she was opening her law office. So I think I mentioned knitting. And she asked if Edna still ran her knitting circles."

Burlap nodded. "Thanks for clarifying. Now, please go ahead. What happened then?"

Becca took him through the full story. Then he asked Ona to recount her version of events, starting from the very beginning. Finally, it was Alice's turn. Her retelling departed from her friends' stories when she herself departed from the Yarn Shoppe, chasing a shadow into the woods.

Burlap said, "So you didn't see the person's face or other distinguishing features?"

Alice shook her head. "Maybe footprints will reveal something?"

"We've searched the area. And we'll continue to search the area. But the North Trail begins next to the Yarn Shoppe, and people cut through the woods or go wandering off to look for mushrooms. The whole place is a confusion of boot prints."

"The person I saw," Alice said, "could it have been the killer?"

Burlap considered the question. He was a quiet, solid kind of man who showed respect to people by listening and taking time to consider their questions. Alice found his style reassuring—a welcome change from Chief Jimbo's inexperience.

He said, "The Yarn Shoppe's window was ajar when the evening began, you said. But after the victim was found dead, the window was wide open. The victim died of a punctured heart caused by a sharpened knitting needle penetrating her back. The knitting needle, made of stainless steel, had been honed to an almost syringe-like sharpness. Could the killer have opened the window and thrown the knitting needle? Well, in theory maybe. But the killer would need to be an uncommonly skilled thrower. The killer would also need to stand at a precise angle to hit the precise point in the back with the needle, so it could bypass bone to reach the heart."

"So the chances of that happening are next to impossible."

"I didn't say that, Miss Hartford. The knitting needle wasn't just filed down a bit—it was honed to perfection. The entry wound suggests a killer adept enough to know the precise place to strike. Up close, an amateur might stab another person in the right spot, but at a distance, throwing the missile, the killer would have to be a pro, especially since it only took one attempt to hit the victim. Having said that, the window provided the right angle to hitting the victim's back, at least based on the placement of the chair." He shook his head. "It's far-fetched. It reminds me of a plot from a Poirot or Lord Peter Wimsey mystery. But *far-fetched* isn't the same as *impossible*."

Alice nodded, appreciating Burlap's openness to possibilities.

"Now, about the suspects inside the store—" she began.

But he cut her off by raising a hand.

"Please, Miss Hartford. I value your insights and your track record of solving mysteries in this town. But I hope you'll agree that my colleagues and I have the resources one needs to solve a serious—and unusual—crime of this nature."

"I was just—"

"Miss Hartford, do we agree?"

He stared at her. He had a kindly but firm expression that said, "You'd better answer me, and the answer better be yes."

Finally, Alice nodded.

"I agree, Captain Burlap. My job is selling books, not catching killers."

Burlap smiled, dimples showing.

"Great."

"Yeah," Alice said. "Great."

CHAPTER 8

*A*t daybreak on Monday morning, Alice took a stroll in the woods.

It was a beautiful spring day with a fresh, dewy chill in the air. Blithedale's Main Street cut through the forested landscape, barely making a dent in the lush foliage. Trees backed onto every business. So you could step off Main Street almost anywhere and enter the woods in seconds.

This morning, Alice thought she'd enjoy a walk along the North Trail. Why not? Wandering around the woods near a crime scene wasn't illegal.

And if I just happen to find something interesting, she thought, *then won't Captain Burlap thank me?*

Crime scene tape festooned the front door of the Yarn Shoppe, though because the store lay secluded among the trees, cars passing would hardly notice it. Clearly, last night's police activity hadn't attracted rubberneckers of the vehicular or pedestrian variety. There wasn't a car or hiker in sight.

The cops weren't on the scene, either. Presumably, they'd

worked long into the night to study the scene before moving on to another crime in the state.

Which left Alice alone.

She wandered around the little building. Around the back, she studied—from a distance, of course—the fateful window. Unruly bushes grew against the building, their thorns clawing at the store's warped shutters. The shadow would've had to press through thorny brambles to get to the window.

She crouched down and peered at the soft ground. Captain Burlap was right: the area around the Yarn Shoppe was a mess of boot prints. She stepped back, then turned and moved farther and farther from the building. She reached the North Trail. Hikers had pounded the ground into hard-packed dirt, leaving fewer prints to study. Crossing the trail, she headed into the woods.

What did she hope to find that Burlap and his officers hadn't found already? A clue to the shadow's identity? It was too much to hope for.

She studied the ground. Did she run to the left or the right? In the dark, she'd hardly had a sense of direction, turning whichever way she sensed the shadow ran in.

Looking back at the Yarn Shoppe, now 50 yards away, she could say with certainty that she hadn't come back this way. The angle was wrong. She remembered the window hadn't been visible when she'd headed back to the store.

Farther to the left, she thought.

She moved across mossy rocks and twisty roots until she came to one she'd swear was the one that had felled her.

When I fell, she thought, *the shadow ran that way.*

She headed in that direction. The rocks grew bigger, the roots gnarlier, and even more brambles joined the massive tree trunks.

Whoever the shadow was, the person had known how to

navigate the woods. They were also fast and agile, flying across this uneven ground without tripping.

She kept an eye on the dirt by her feet.

"There," she muttered to herself.

Was that half a boot print? Or maybe a hoof had made the indentation? There was no shortage of deer to make such marks in the dirt. Yes, probably just a hoof print.

She moved forward, and then came to the North Trail.

She let out a curse. She'd never be able to track the shadow if the person had followed the trail.

Which was the smart thing to do, she thought. *After all, once the killer hit the trail, they'd move even faster, while I was back there floundering on the ground.*

She was about to step onto the trail when she saw it.

She crouched down.

A boot had made a deep imprint in the soft ground where it rose to the trail. She could picture her quarry now. The shadow had reached the trail and then stepped onto the incline, pressing deep into the dirt.

Alice brought out her phone and took pictures of the imprint.

She was lucky: the ground was still soft from the recent spring showers and the person's step was so firmly pressed into the earth that the dirt had captured the boot tread in detail. As she snapped photos, she leaned closer.

Is that—?

She smiled to herself. Yes, indeed. It was a logo from the bottom of the boot.

It looked like an ox.

After snapping a few more photos, she opened her browser on her phone and googled "boots ox logo." She found boots with special patches stitched on, including one of an ox. None of them had treads with that distinctive ox logo.

Soon, the search turned up completely irrelevant results, like a ranch in Wyoming where you could adopt an ox.

Like looking for a needle in a haystack. Then, with a shudder, she thought: *A knitting needle.*

She straightened up. Her thighs and calves were aching.

She found a nearby tree to lean against as she tried other search terms. And then had an idea: what if they were work boots? She typed in another search. And after scrolling through more results, she found it.

Sturdy Steer Workwear. Its logo was an ox wearing boots. The company produced workwear, primarily boots and shoes but also some water resistant jackets and hats.

Next, she searched on "Blithedale" and "Sturdy Steer Workwear." Nothing. No hits at all.

She broadened her search to include nearby "Tilbury Town."

Bingo.

Not the top result, but close to the top, was a press release announcing a supplier partnership between Sturdy Steer Workwear and Ridgeway Cleaning.

Alice smiled to herself. Not only was she familiar with Ridgeway Cleaning—the company had sponsored the Blithedale Christmas Fair—but she also knew someone working there who could tell her more about Sturdy Steer, and whether one of their employees would wear the boot that had made the imprint here in the woods.

It's a long shot, she told herself. *But it's a clue.*

She scrolled through her contacts until she found the number for Ridgeway Cleaning. She hit dial. After talking to the receptionist, she got transferred to her friend Mohammad.

"Alice," he said, genuine joy in his voice. "What can I do for you?"

"Mo," she said. "I'm looking for some intel on boots."

"Boots?" He laughed. He had one of those big, booming belly laughs that made other people laugh, too. He said, "You're going to have to explain."

She told him what she needed to know.

Mohammad said, "That's right. All our work boots come from Sturdy Steer. We have an exclusive supplier agreement with them. How come?"

"Oh, just curious."

Mohammad laughed again. "I know all about your curiosity, Alice. In Arabic, I would tell you, '*Alfudul qatl alqatati.*'"

"What does it mean?"

"'Curiosity,'" he said, "'killed the cat.'"

CHAPTER 9

*A*fter her walk in the woods, Alice headed for the What the Dickens Diner for breakfast. Ona was already sitting at the counter, enjoying her coffee, while Becca stood on the other side. Alice was about to launch into an explanation of the boot print she'd found when she saw Becca was holding a postcard in her hand.

"Another one?" Alice said as she slid onto the stool next to Ona's.

Becca nodded and handed over the card.

Like the others, its design and choice of subject were so generic as to be forgettable: the Statue of Liberty, the Golden Gate Bridge, Mount Rushmore, next to big bold letters that said, "America." Another image showed a Greyhound bus, and suddenly she had Simon & Garfunkel's song "America" playing in her head.

She turned the postcard over and read the typewritten quote: "A good friend will always stab you in the front."

The skin prickled on the back of her neck. She looked at Becca, then at Ona.

Becca said, "Oscar Wilde again."

"And not to point out the obvious," Ona said, "but it mentions stabbing."

Now the poison-pen postcards didn't seem so harmless.

"Do you think Edna's killer sent the cards?" Alice asked.

"This one is postmarked two days ago. By then, the killer must've planned out the murder. So, yes, it's possible."

As they were puzzling over the postcard, Beau came to the counter and said good morning and ordered a coffee. He glanced over and said, "Another one, huh? Me too." He dug into his jacket and pulled out a crumpled postcard and put it on the counter.

It was another generic tourism postcard, this one showcasing the Pacific Northwest, with photos of Mount Rainier, Seattle's Space Needle, and the Multnomah Falls in Oregon, each one labeled.

On the back was a typewritten message: "The worst thing about some men is that when they are not drunk, they are sober."

Alice's chest tightened, and she glanced at Beau, worried about how the message had affected him. Beau was an alcoholic and had struggled with drinking for most of his adulthood. It was only recently that he joined Alcoholics Anonymous and transformed his life, returning to Blithedale from his hermit life in the woods to take control of the family business, the theater.

But Beau didn't seem affected by the message.

"The quote is by William Butler Yeats," he said. "And, Alice, I can see by the way you're looking at me, you're worried. Don't be. If someone wants to insult me by calling me 'sober,' they can go right ahead. I've heard worse. What I'm wondering is why I've inspired this kind of nastiness."

"That's what I was thinking, too," Becca said. "I've had unhappy customers who would write nasty reviews online, trying to get back at me for some perceived insult. Which is what I assumed this was. But now I'm not so sure…"

Alice compared the two postcards.

"How many did you receive, Beau?"

He shrugged. "Five or six over the course of two or three weeks."

"Anyone else get them?"

"Lorraine. Sandy Spiegel. Mayor MacDonald. Todd Townsend."

"Susan, too," Becca said, referring to the diner's waitress.

Alice said, "What about Andrea at Bonsai & Pie? Or Thor at the Woodlander Bar?"

Beau shook his head. So did Becca.

Becca said, "I spoke with Esther at the consignment store, and she didn't get any either."

"And I didn't get any cards," Alice said. "Nor did Ona."

"What's your theory?" Ona asked.

"I don't know yet. Becca, Beau, Susan, Lorraine, Sandy, the mayor, and Todd Townsend. What sets them apart from me, you, Esther, and Andrea?"

Ona shrugged. "Apart from the fact that we're relatively new to Blithedale? Nothing, I guess."

A light seemed to brighten in Alice's mind and she nudged Ona.

"You're a genius, Ona."

"I am?"

Because Ona was right: all the people who'd received poison-pen postcards had lived in Blithedale for most of their lives.

CHAPTER 10

*A*fter opening Wonderland Books for the day, Alice struggled to decide whether to call Captain Burlap. As she shelved books, she considered what she knew. Was it even worth bothering him about the little she'd discovered? The information about the Sturdy Steer boot print might be nothing, after all. As Burlap himself had pointed out, the woods were full of impressions left by passersby. Until Alice had more than a hunch to go on, how helpful was it for her to throw ideas at the state police investigator?

And then there's the poison-pen postcard writer, she thought, as she stood on a stool to slip another copy of *Crime and Punishment* by Dostoevsky onto the top shelf. Nearby, she made space for *The Count of Monte Cristo* by Dumas.

The person sending the postcards is mean-spirited, for sure, and has a serious chip on their shoulder...

But, she had to admit to herself, apart from that vague—and maybe coincidental—reference to stabbing, there was no evidence that the writer and the killer were the same person.

The door to the bookstore opened and someone came in.

Alice got down from the stool, turning around to greet the customer. And froze.

"Oh," she said. "Hi."

It was the mystery woman from Main Street—the one she was sure she knew from somewhere. The woman was wearing a light-blue jacket with a hoodie underneath it.

"Alice?" the woman said, and took a step back, visibly shocked. Then she cocked her head, as if unsure if she'd recognized the right person. "No way. Alice Hartford?"

Then the memory—and realization of who this was—came rushing back over Alice. "Simone? Simone Springer?"

Alice laughed, and an awkward moment followed where neither of them knew what to do. She took a step forward and stopped. Simone made a move, too, though more timidly. Then Alice, pushing caution aside, plunged forward and threw her arms around her old friend.

"Simone," she said, hugging her.

When they broke apart, Alice smiled. "When I saw you in the street, I knew I recognized you from somewhere, but I couldn't place you. That was because the last time I saw you, we were kids. How many years has it been? Twenty?"

"When you moved from Blithedale," Simone said, nodding. Then her face lost all its joy. "Around the time your mom…"

Alice nodded. "After she died, I lost my way for a long time, but I'm back now."

Simone looked around. "And you own a bookstore. Hey, is that a copy of Clyde Digby's latest romance novel? Great escapism. Though my favorites are still the classics. Digby can't compete with the Brontë sisters."

"I remember you as crazy precocious, reading *Wuthering Heights* at 9 years old."

"In an abridged version."

"Still."

They talked about the books they adored. As childhood friends, they'd spent hours discussing the topic—swapping books and dreaming about what it would be like to inhabit the imaginary worlds they loved to visit: Narnia, Oz, and Neverland.

"And Wonderland," Simone said, "like your bookstore."

"My big dream come true. Or my tiny dream, if you judge it by the size of this place. But tell me about you: When did you leave? Are you back? How's your family?"

Simone turned away. "Fine. Everything's fine. I got a job at a facility services company in Tilbury Town—so I'm close, but not all the way back to Blithedale. My dad's last congregation was in Arizona, but he's now retired and he and mom have stayed down there in the warm weather." She studied the shelves—or pretended to. Alice sensed the topic made her uncomfortable. After a moment of silence, Simone said, "My sister's gone."

"Oh, Simone, I'm so sorry. I had no idea."

"Jenny was never the same after what happened…"

Alice searched her memory for some idea of what Simone was referring to, but came up blank. She said, "I'm sorry, Simone. I'm not sure I know what happened."

Simone gave her a sharp, appraising look. Then sighed. "Well, why would you? It began around the time you were still in Blithedale, but then you left, and everything exploded."

"Exploded?"

"They accused Jenny of stealing money."

The mention of stealing money sparked a memory. Yes, there had been some trouble with Jenny, hadn't there? And now that she thought about it, it might've involved the Yarn Shoppe somehow. Or was she superimposing her current preoccupation with Edna's store onto an incident from 20 years ago? So many memories from that period were gone, lost in the maelstrom of emotions around her mom's cancer diagnosis.

Simone said, "Jenny was innocent, but no one believed her. After we moved away from Blithedale, halfway across the country, she struggled with anger—real rage—and couldn't seem to settle down. She dropped out of high school. She went from job to job. Then—"

She shook her head, clamped her mouth shut.

Alice put a hand on her arm. "Hey, if you don't want to talk about it…"

"I don't." She shook Alice's hand off. Then took a deep breath and said, "Anyway, I just dropped in to look around the bookshop. I didn't realize it was yours—I didn't even know you were back in Blithedale."

"But now that you do," Alice said, "I hope we can grab a cup of coffee sometime."

"Yeah, all right."

Alice had hoped for a more enthusiastic response, but the topic of her sister seemed to have muted Simone.

Simone slipped a pair of sunglasses on, and it felt as if she was raising a wall between them. She said, "I'd better get back to Tilbury Town. My shift starts soon. See you around, Alice."

She turned on her heels and headed for the door. The lettering on the back of Simone's blue jacket said, "Ridgeway Cleaning." What had Simone said? "I got a job at a facility services company in Tilbury Town." Alice hadn't made the connection, but it made sense: Ridgeway Cleaning was the most successful facility services company in town.

But that wasn't the biggest surprise.

Looking down, Alice caught sight of Simone's muddy boots, and her stomach twisted.

No…

The back of the boots had a logo on it, all too familiar by now: an ox wearing boots.

Sturdy Steer work boots.

For a long time after Simone had left, Alice stood rooted to the floor, staring at the door. Then she dug out her phone and found the business card. She dialed the number.

"Captain Burlap," she said when he answered. "I have some important information about Edna's murder."

CHAPTER 11

*A*lice got little sleep that night. The Colonel Brandon Suite's cozy canopy bed offered no comfort. She tossed and turned as if the Pemberley Inn's sheets were made of horsehair. Her mind wouldn't settle down. It engaged her in an endless dialogue, ping-ponging thoughts back and forth.

I shouldn't have called Captain Burlap.

You did the right thing—even if the evidence means nothing, he needed to know.

But Simone...

Well, those muddy boots...

Still, Simone was always a good kid, a stickler for doing the right thing. She'd never kill someone.

Are you sure about that? Do you really know her that well?

Exhaustion must've dragged her down into sleep, because she woke up at dawn, with the sheets twisted around her legs and the pillow over her head.

She groaned and rolled out of bed.

I shouldn't have called Captain Burlap, she thought again. *Or should I?*

She showered and dressed and headed downstairs.

Ona was behind the reception counter, typing on the computer.

"Morning," she said. "Ready to head over to the diner for breakfast?"

Alice nodded. Ona glanced at her with her one visible eye, but said nothing.

They walked to the diner. Along the way, Ona commented on things they passed on Main Street, including Trudy's law office. A sign in the window said, "Open."

"Apparently, Mayor MacDonald is excited," Ona said. "First our town gets a lawyer, he said. Next comes a bank. Then growth will really take off."

Alice nodded, thinking only of Simone.

When they got to the diner and Ona pushed open the door, she said, "Go find a booth. I'll order us some coffee and overnight oats at the counter."

Alice found an empty booth and slipped onto the leatherette seat.

Burlap needed to know...

No, you put Simone in an unfair position...

She buried her face in her hands.

Then made a decision. She dug out her phone and redialed the number.

Captain Burlap answered on the first ring.

"Alice," he said, sounding winded. Or excited. "Glad you called."

"Captain Burlap, about Simone—"

"Yes, you were right," he said, cutting her off. "I did some digging. Simone Springer's big sister, Jenny, died in a car accident last year. About 20 years ago, Jenny was accused of several burglaries in Blithedale. Here's the thing: one of the places she hit—the last one, in fact—was the Yarn Shoppe.

But she was caught red-handed. Of course, she insisted she was innocent. The incident drove the family out of town, and it seems to have shaped Jenny's life after that, which then traced a steady downhill trajectory."

Alice said, "But Simone said her sister was innocent—"

"Exactly. She's got a clear motive: years ago, Edna accused Jenny of theft, and now Simone believes her sister was unjustly accused. Then, a few days ago, she was snooping around Blithedale. Maybe she was planning the attack. And thanks to your sleuthing, we can place her near the scene of the crime, even if we can't prove that she stood at that window. Not yet, anyway." He chuckled. "I underestimated what you could do, Alice. Thank you for ignoring me and taking another look at the area around the crime scene. Your sleuthing has been genuinely useful. Now, what was it you wanted to say?"

"Simone," Alice said, feeling diminished by Burlap's enthusiasm. "She couldn't have killed Edna."

"Oh? Why not? Does she have an alibi? I checked with Ridgeway Cleaning, and she got off her shift with plenty of time to get to the Yarn Shoppe on the night of the murder. Do you know something I don't know?"

"Only that Simone isn't the kind of person who'd murder someone."

Silence at the other end.

Burlap's voice went soft. "Alice, I understand this isn't easy. She's an old friend of yours. You never want someone you've cared about—maybe still care about—to reveal a dark side. But trust me, I see this all the time in my work."

"But—"

"Let the facts speak for themselves. This case may move in a different direction. Or the facts may all point to Simone. It's too early to tell."

After hanging up, Alice thought about what he'd said. He'd sounded sympathetic and reasonable. But he'd also sounded thrilled to have a solid lead. He might say that the case could move in a different direction, but her gut told her that Captain Burlap liked the idea that Simone was the killer.

Ona and Becca arrived with coffee and breakfast, and Ona sat down. Becca remained standing—there were too many customers in the diner for her to take a break.

Ona poured Alice a cup of coffee and said, "All right. Spit it out. You look like you've been up half the night, and you're acting as if someone told you that book reading's been abolished."

Alice wrapped her fingers around the warm cup and drank the black coffee, savoring the strong taste.

"It's about Simone Springer."

Last night, she'd filled them in on her discovery, and now she went back over the details of her encounter with Simone, the apparent clues connecting her with Edna's murder, and then her decision to call Captain Burlap.

"But then I started doubting myself," she said.

"Because you don't want Simone to be the killer?" Ona said.

"Because I *know* Simone can't be the killer."

She explained Captain Burlap's theory about Simone's motive, detailing the story he'd dug up about the burglaries.

"If Simone believes Jenny was innocent, maybe there's something to it," she said. "Besides, the whole thing about Simone's motive is absurd. I mean, if he's right, Jenny allegedly stole from many stores. So why would Simone, in retribution, kill Edna and not one of the other business owners?"

Ona shrugged. "Didn't he say that Edna was the one who caught her?"

"Not Edna," Becca said.

"There," Alice said. "See? Edna wasn't even the one who caught Jenny stealing. So why would Simone target Edna? I don't believe it. Besides, as a kid, Simone would immediately tell a parent if a friend stole a piece of candy or cheated on a homework assignment. She had a robust sense of right and wrong."

"Last time you saw her, you were, what, 9 years old?" Ona said. "How can you know what she's like as an adult?"

"I just know she couldn't do such a thing. And I'm going to prove it."

"You are?"

Alice drained her coffee. Her heart was beating fast. Either it was the caffeine taking effect or she was feeling a renewed sense of purpose.

Captain Burlap himself had said her sleuthing was useful. So she would make herself useful by investigating Edna's murder.

She sat up straight and shoved the empty coffee cup aside.

"Look, I'll prove that Simone didn't kill Edna. I'll find the actual killer."

Ona grinned. "Oh, well, in that case, I totally agree with whatever you say. No way Simone could've done it. Let's investigate."

"You're just enthusiastic because we get to sneak around like Nancy Drew."

"And you aren't?"

Alice turned to Becca, who'd remained quiet. It wasn't like her. Becca, meeting Alice's gaze, said, "Be careful. I don't want you to get hurt."

"Don't worry, we won't," Alice said. "It'll take more than a knitting needle to pierce my heart."

Becca, nodding slowly, regarded Alice with a sad look in her eyes.

"That's what worries me, Alice. Your heart."

Then a customer called her away, leaving Alice puzzled by her comment.

But only for a moment. Because she had a mystery to solve, and she knew who she wanted to talk to first about Edna's death.

CHAPTER 12

*H*ildegarde York lived in a cabin in the woods north of the town center. Wednesday afternoon, after Alice closed Wonderland for the day, Ona drove them in her pickup truck and parked at the end of Hildegarde's short dirt drive. A hiking trail crossed the nearby road, snaking into the woods.

"Which trail is that?" Alice asked Ona.

"The North Trail."

"So you can walk straight down to the Yarn Shoppe from here?"

"Not exactly 'straight,' but yes, if you follow the trail, it'll lead you to Main Street by the Yarn Shoppe."

They approached the cabin, but before they'd reached the low porch, the door opened. Hildegarde ducked down under the lintel and waited for them, her arms crossed.

"Why are you here?"

She blocked the doorway, clearly unwilling to invite them in. But Alice had prepared for this. Remembering the woman's penchant for quoting the Bible, she'd googled some verses.

"'Do not forget to show hospitality to strangers,'" Alice said, "'for by so doing some people have shown hospitality to angels without knowing it.'"

Hildegarde stared daggers at her. Then said, "I prefer the King James version: 'Be not forgetful to entertain strangers: for thereby some have entertained angels unawares.' But it amounts to the same. Come in."

She ducked into the cabin, and Alice didn't wait for her to change her mind. She followed. Ona came close behind her.

The cabin comprised a small kitchen and living space, plus a bathroom and a bedroom. Its decorations were spartan, bordering on monastic. A big wooden crucifix dominated one wall. Another held a framed print of Christ suffering on the cross.

A bookshelf drew Alice's attention. Books were a promising sign. Homes without books made Alice suspicious, if not uncomfortable. What did it say about a person who didn't keep a single book within reach? It was far easier to understand how people could hoard so many books that they risked burying their furniture—and themselves.

On closer inspection, the bookshelf she was nearest contained only Bibles. There must've been a dozen different translations in various editions, from the King James Version to the New Revised Standard. The bookshelf next to it showed a more diverse selection, with texts by St. Augustine and Thomas Aquinas and biographies of Martin Luther and Calvin.

"No romance novels by Clyde Digby, I see," Ona muttered.

Hildegarde stared at them.

"Well?" she said.

Alice noted she didn't offer them coffee or any other refreshments. She'd let them into her home, but she didn't want them to stay.

"We wanted to ask you about Edna," Alice said.

"The police asked me already."

"Were you and Edna friends?"

"We weren't enemies, if that's what you're getting at."

While Alice talked, Ona continued to study the bookshelves. She moved on to a desk next to them. Occasionally, Hildegarde glanced toward Ona, frowning, but she said nothing about Ona's nosiness.

Alice said, "You didn't sign up for the knitting club. You simply showed up. Why?"

"Thessalonians bids us do our own business and work with our own hands."

"So," Alice said, trying to make sense of what Hildegarde said, "you joined a knitting club to work with your hands?"

"What else?"

"Well, you could knit at home. You didn't need to join a club."

Hildegarde didn't comment. She stared stonily at Alice.

Then Ona said, "Wow, that's a lot of postcards you've got."

"And so?"

"Just unusual to see so many postcards."

"The church relief funds sell them and I buy them."

"I'm terrible at writing letters," Ona said. "Do you actually write cards and mail them?"

"Of course I do." Hildegarde sighed. "Even if few respond to me."

"Who do you write to—family…or maybe friends here in town?"

"I have a few relatives out of state. And I have friends who used to belong to the Blithedale church. They moved years ago."

"And you write to them using one of these pens?"

Ona gestured at the writing tools on the desk. She looked around, scanning the rest of the cabin. Alice could guess what she was looking for: a typewriter. There could be one tucked away in the bedroom, of course, but none was visible from where they stood.

"A pen, of course. What else would I use?" Hildegarde's frown deepened. "What do my postcards have to do with Edna's death?"

Ona shrugged. "Just curious."

Alice brought them back to the topic at hand. "Did you see anything unusual that night?"

"I saw an old friend murdered. Is that unusual enough?"

"I mean, did you see anyone do anything suspicious?"

"Your questions are suspicious."

"We're trying to help."

Hildegarde grew tight-lipped, her mouth a thin, hard line. She said nothing, simply staring hard at Alice, and Alice got uncomfortable under her gaze.

"Well, I guess we've enjoyed your hospitality long enough," she muttered.

She and Ona stepped outside. They were a few paces beyond the porch, when Hildegarde spoke behind them.

"One of the women has sinned and fallen short of the glory of God."

"Who hasn't?" Alice shot back. "It doesn't make someone a killer."

"This woman did not belong there. She hated Edna."

"Lillian?" Alice said.

Hildegarde didn't confirm or deny it. "You asked if someone acted suspicious. Look at the women who joined that knitting club. They all had reasons to hate Edna, but one more so than the others..."

Hildegarde ducked back inside her cabin and shut the door with a firm thump, punctuating her last word.

Lillian, Alice thought.

It wasn't much to go on. But it would have to do.

CHAPTER 13

*L*illian McGlinty's home was impossible to miss. Most Blithedale homes would be described as modest, but on a street with some of the town's largest houses, the McGlinty residence deserved the term "mansion." It even had a wrought-iron gate with the bars curved into an artful "McG" on either side. An intercom to the left and a video camera above it suggested that the McGlintys appreciated security.

Leaning out of the window of her pickup, Ona pressed the button. The intercom hissed softly as it amplified a man's voice.

"Yes?"

"We're here to see Lillian McGlinty."

"No, you're not."

Ona glanced over at Alice. She tried a different tack.

"We'd like to see Lillian, if you'll be so kind."

"Mother isn't taking visitors. Move on or I'll make you."

The soft hiss cut out. The conversation was over.

"Friendly guy," Ona said.

"'Mother'? I didn't know there was a McGlinty, Jr."

"Now we know. And we know that 'Mother' won't see us. So what do we do with that knowledge?"

Alice wasn't sure. Ona put the pickup in reverse and backed away from the gate, swinging into the street. A man emerged from a driveway up ahead, raising a hand in a wave.

As he came toward them, the sycamores casting long afternoon shadows across the man, Alice realized it was Beau. His house was down the street. He must've spotted them from afar.

He leaned against Ona's window and smiled.

"Tried to charm your way into Fort Knox?"

"Tried and failed," Alice said.

"Why don't you see if there's a window you can climb through?"

Alice felt her face grow warm with a blush. Beau, now grinning at his own joke, was referring to the time she'd broken into his house to look for clues to his sister's death.

"Anyway," Beau continued, "you don't want to mess with Cullen McGlinty. He's a real piece of work."

"What makes you say that?" Ona asked.

"I heard through the grapevine that he's a bully. And it's not just gossip. Someone got an actual restraining order on him—or was it a cease-and-desist?" He scratched his chin, thinking. "It's one or the other."

"It's his mom we want to talk to."

"Ah, Lillian. Not the friendliest neighbor on the block. But she likes us all to think she's the most important. When her husband, Bill, was alive, she acted like they were royalty. Since he died, though, she mostly stays at home. I see Cullen come and go more often than I see her. I was surprised she came to Edna's."

Alice said, "Given how hostile she was toward Edna, it surprised me, too."

"It is strange," Beau said. "They used to be thick as thieves, those three—Edna, Jolene, and Lillian—but they had a falling out."

"What kind of falling out?"

Beau shrugged. "I don't know the details. Or don't remember." His comment reminded Alice of the years he'd spent drinking himself into an oblivion. He said, "But it probably involved a guy. Becca may know. After all, if a piece of gossip passes through Blithedale, it makes a pit stop at the diner. Or it pauses at the public library. If Becca doesn't know, I bet Lorraine does."

CHAPTER 14

$\mathcal{N}$othing Beau had noticed on Sunday night helped with the investigation. And when Alice and Ona, grabbing a bite to eat at the diner, asked Becca about the conflict between Edna, Jolene, and Lillian, she said she couldn't remember the exact details. Then she hurried away to take a customer's order.

"Is Becca acting weird?" Alice asked Ona.

"What do you mean 'weird'?"

"Feels like she's avoiding us."

More specifically, Alice thought, *Becca seems to be avoiding me.*

In fact, when they talked about Edna's murder, Becca looked at Ona but struggled to make eye contact with Alice. What the heck was going on?

After finishing dinner—baked salmon with a yoghurt sauce over a bed of arugula—Alice and Ona got back in the pickup truck and drove into the woods. Alice had called Lorraine and learned that she was meeting her best friend, Sandy Spiegel, at the Woodlander Bar. Alice and Ona agreed to go meet them in person.

The Woodlander Bar, one of Ona's tiny houses, sat in a small clearing in the woods. A gravel parking lot provided ample space for cars, though the bar itself could only accommodate a few people. Instead, most patrons sat in the outdoor area under a wide awning. Across from the bar lay the recently opened restaurant, Under the Greenwood Tree.

After parking and getting out of the pickup truck, Alice and Ona headed to the tables shared between the bar and the restaurant. Patio heaters cut the chill in the air. The tables were nearly all occupied by patrons enjoying drinks from the Woodlander or eating dinner from Under the Greenwood Tree, or both.

"Alice, Ona," Lorraine called out, waving from the far end. "Over here."

They made their way past the tables, greeting people they knew along the way. Mayor MacDonald, dressed in his usual Mark Twain-like white suit, smiled at Alice and pointedly ignored Ona.

"When will that man grow up and stop treating you like an enemy?" Alice asked Ona.

Ona laughed. "When he realizes tiny houses won't ruin the real estate market in Blithedale."

"Will he ever?"

"Well, he made an exception with your bookstore, didn't he? Great oaks from tiny acorns do grow."

"And what do tiny houses grow from?"

Ona laughed. "My hands?"

Lorraine greeted the two of them warmly and invited them to sit down. Sandy said hello too. With her broad shoulders, she took up half the table. She was as tall as some of the tallest basketball players Alice had ever seen.

Lorraine and Sandy were drinking creamy Brandy Alexanders. Alice offered to grab drinks from inside as Ona settled onto a seat. She wandered over to the tiny house bar.

There was a line at the bar inside, but it didn't take long before it cleared and the bartender and owner, Thor, called out her name. She stepped up to the bar, leaning on it.

"What can I get you?"

"Two glasses of white wine, please."

Thor smiled, grabbed a bottle of white, uncorked it, and poured into two glasses. He was a handsome Danish man with long, blonde hair, a kind of idealized version of a viking. Alice wasn't attracted to him—he wasn't her type, if there was such a thing—but that didn't mean she didn't enjoy looking at him.

"Here you go," he said, handing her the glasses of wine. "By the way, I heard about the woman who owned the Yarn Shoppe. Terrible news."

"Did you know her?"

He shook his head. "But her friend, Lillian, seemed deeply upset by it. She's a regular. She told me what a shock it was to lose one of her oldest friends."

"She said that? I'm surprised. I saw her around Edna, and they didn't seem to get along."

Thor shrugged. "She seemed genuinely upset. She even shared regret that she hadn't reconnected with Edna sooner."

"Bartenders and priests—people tell you everything."

"Don't forget hairdressers. My mom's a hairdresser, and she knows half of Copenhagen's secrets. But about Lillian, you don't need to take my word for it. She's sitting right over there."

Alice swung around, surprised to see Lillian sitting in a corner with a young man. This was her opportunity to talk to Lillian about Edna's death.

Alice crossed the floor of the tiny house, which didn't take long, and stood by Lillian's table.

"Hi, Lillian—got a minute?"

Lillian gave Alice a cold, disinterested look. But there was something else in those eyes too, an uncertainty held steady by discipline, maybe even fear.

The young man shot to his feet. "Back off, lady."

He had flinty, blue eyes, and a trimmed mustache and side-part that—combined with a white shirt and black tie—made him look like a time traveler from 1930s or 40s Germany. His mouth turned down in a morose frown.

Alice had a strange thought:

So this is the sort of young man who would've joined the National Socialist Party.

He came at her. Something about his gaze and his stance —sheer animal brutishness—made her take a step back. He didn't need to raise a hand to convince her he was used to intimidation.

"I just came to pay my respects."

"Bull," he said. "You came to snoop."

She craned her neck to the side, just enough to glimpse Lillian over Cullen's right shoulder. "Hope to talk sometime, Lillian."

"Don't bet on it," Cullen growled.

Alice didn't tempt fate. She backed away from him and then retreated.

Near the bar, Thor stopped her.

"You all right? Was he bothering you?"

"Don't worry about it, Thor. I'm fine."

Alice left the tiny house. Outside, she let out a breath, surprised by how relieved she was to escape Cullen's orbit. The guy was scary. Her gut told her he didn't have the kinds of boundaries that most people did. She preferred not to spend time with people like that.

She joined Ona, Lorraine, and Sandy, handing Ona her glass of white wine and then sitting down. They were in the middle of an engaged conversation, leaving her no chance to tell them about her interaction with Lillian and Cullen.

"Fred Burr," Ona told Alice. "That's who got between the three friends."

"Better start at the beginning," Alice said.

Lorraine said, "Edna, Jolene, and Lillian used to be best friends. They grew up in Blithedale, went to school together, even attended the same church."

"The same church as Hildegarde?"

"There weren't many to choose from back then," Lorraine said, nodding. "In the early days, Lillian had a longtime boyfriend, Fred Burr. He left her and began dating Edna."

"Let me guess," Alice said, "then he left Edna for Jolene?"

"Yes, but not before marrying Edna."

"Whoa, what?"

"Yes, Edna Lawner was Edna Burr for 20 years. She suspected Fred had an affair with Lillian and feared he'd run off with her. But instead, Fred left Edna for Jolene, and they got married. So Lillian never forgave Edna or Jolene for stealing Fred. She hated them both."

"How did Edna feel about Jolene 'stealing' Fred from her?"

"Enraged. She hated Jolene. And she still blamed Lillian for the affair."

Alice ran a hand across her forehead. "This is making me dizzy. And then what happened?"

"Then Fred died."

"Leaving the three estranged friends behind."

"Exactly."

And with Fred gone, she thought, there was only one thing left to do: get revenge.

CHAPTER 15

The next day, Alice and Ona were leaning against the counter at Wonderland Books, hands wrapped around warm cups of tea while they talked about Edna's murder.

"Why revenge?" Ona said, blowing steam off the top of her tea. "With Fred gone, maybe they could bury old grievances and rekindle their friendship. Frankly, I don't like these stories about women fighting like cats over a man—they feel outdated."

"I agree. Not my favorite, either. But I don't think it's as simple as that."

Alice had given her revenge theory some more thought during the night, and she had an idea to share. But with beautiful spring weather outside, the door to the bookshop stood open and customers wandered in, demanding Alice's attention. A man asked her if they had Clyde Digby's novel *Three Sins and a Duke* ("For a friend," he said and blushed), and Alice dug out a used copy she hadn't priced yet and bagged it for him with a smile and an assurance that anyone

—men or women—could enjoy a good, steamy romance novel.

Then she turned back to Ona to explain her idea.

"I'm thinking Jolene might've joined the knitting club to rekindle their friendship. After all, she was the one who got Fred in the end. With him gone, she might feel lonely. She might long to reconnect with her two best friends."

"Former best friends. I don't think Edna seemed up for it. She was pretty cold toward Jolene."

"I agree. And Lillian was hostile to both of them. She seemed to show up because she somehow heard that Jolene was going to be there. Plus, there's Cullen McGlinty—"

Someone said, "What about Cullen McGlinty?"

Trudy strode into the store, looking around, as if on a mission. She didn't wait for an answer to her question. She spotted something in a bookshelf, headed over and grabbed a paperback, then found another, and another.

At the counter, she put down a stack of books. Alice saw they were all legal thrillers by popular authors—John Grisham, Scott Turow, and Robert Bailey.

"For my waiting room," she explained as she paid for the books. "Men like a page-turner thriller."

"Women, too," Alice said.

"For the women, I've got People Magazine, fashion stuff, even a knitting magazine. Oh, which reminds me, you mentioned Cullen McGlinty."

"Because he enjoys knitting?" Ona asked with a wry smile.

"Because of Edna's murder, which made me think of Lillian, and that leads us to Cullen. But I wasn't the one who mentioned him. You did."

"Alice had a confrontation with Cullen."

"Well, he did all the confronting," Alice said. "I did the walking away."

Trudy smiled that big-toothed smile. "He's got a history of being a tough guy."

"Oh?"

"When I worked at a law firm in Tilbury Town, they helped a client put out a cease-and-desist letter to warn him off. He was intimidating the client."

"I'm guessing attorney ethics keep you from telling us who the client was."

"You better believe it. A lawyer's only as good as her reputation." Trudy gathered up her books. "But I'm not divulging confidential information by telling you Cullen used to work as a security guard at Tilbury Services, a competitor to Ridgeway Cleaning."

Alice and Ona exchange glances. Ridgeway Cleaning again.

"Thanks, Trudy," Alice said. "That's really helpful."

"By the way, Captain Burlap came by my office and grilled me about the night Edna was killed. He mentioned her funeral tomorrow. I'm going. You want to come with me? I'm sure it'll be a blast."

Alice winced. Trudy had the social grace of a bull in a china shop. But Alice shared her interest in the funeral. She wanted to see who else turned up and how they behaved. They agreed to meet Trudy at the cemetery tomorrow.

After she left, Ona shook her head. "I can see why Trudy had a hard time making friends as a kid. She's about as sensitive as a wrecking ball."

But Alice was only half-listening. Ona nudged her.

"Hey," she said. "You're miles away."

Alice nodded. "I was thinking…"

"Say no more." Ona checked her watch. "Closing time soon. We can jump in my pickup and be in Tilbury Town in an hour. I say we try to meet with Mohammad in person. He may know a thing or two about Cullen."

Alice smiled and put an arm around Ona. "You're a mind reader."

CHAPTER 16

*A*s Ona had guessed, it took them about an hour to get to Tilbury Town after Alice shut Wonderland Books for the day. The pickup pulled into the parking lot and the two of them got out. The glass-and-steel office building had large letters on the side that said, "Ridgeway Cleaning."

Inside, the space was spotless and the receptionist, equally clean and groomed, greeted them with a polished smile. After they explained they had an appointment, she made a call.

"Mohammad will be with you in a moment."

She pointed out a nearby waiting area—an arrangement of leather chairs and sofas interspersed with office plants—and suggested Alice and Ona should take a seat.

"Would you like a glass of water or coffee or tea while you wait?"

But at that moment, Mohammad arrived. He gave Alice and Ona a big smile and shook their hands. Ever since catching a killer together, they'd become friends. Moham-mad, who used to insist on calling everyone "mister" and "miss," had become informal, even encouraging Alice and Ona to call him "Mo."

He said, "Coffee? You know how good our coffee is."

He went to a nearby coffee station to make them Americanos. A couple of minutes later, they found seats together in the waiting area and sipped their hot coffees.

"Tell me," he said. "What can I do for you? You were very mysterious on the phone."

"Cullen McGlinty," Alice said.

Mohammad grimaced. "A name I don't like. What has he done now?"

"So you know him?"

"Unfortunately, yes. He works for our main competitor, Tilbury Services. TS, we call them. At Ridgeway, we don't offer security services, so we have a few clients where we manage cleaning, engineering, and facility management, and then subcontract security from TS. But TS also offers other facility services, and somehow Cullen became convinced that if we, Ridgeway, did poorly on the contract, TS would win the full contract instead." Mohammad sighed. "So he tried to sabotage our work."

"Sabotage?"

"First small stuff. He left trash in wastepaper baskets to suggest our cleaners had forgotten to empty them. He removed coffee cups from coffee stations, annoying the client. Then bigger things. He messed with electrical wiring to make our engineers seem incompetent. It could've caused a fire. But I caught him."

"How did he react?"

Mohammad laughed. "Not good. He threatened me. He threatened my family." Mohammad frowned. "Intimidation isn't new to me. I experienced horrific things back in my home country. But I know I don't have to accept it here, even —especially—when the man insults me and my family."

"Did you contact the police?"

"It was a delicate matter. The managers at TS didn't like the situation. None of us wanted to create problems for the client. So I spoke with Ridgeway's lawyers, and they sent a letter to Mr. McGlinty to warn him he must stop."

"And did he?"

"He left me alone. But TS fired him, and I hear he threatened his manager. It resulted in Sheriff Cutter showing up. After that, I think, Mr. McGlinty learned his lesson." Mohammad cocked his head, eyeing Alice with concern. "Alice, if you cross this man's path, you must be careful. He's a bad man."

"I'll be careful," Alice promised. "Tell me something else, Mo. Do security guards at TS wear boots from Sturdy Steer?"

Mohammad shook his head. "They use another supplier for their workwear."

"But since TS's security services were subcontracted to Ridgeway, would Cullen have worn Ridgeway's uniform and boots?"

"No, our agreement with TS was that their staff wouldn't wear our uniforms. Cullen would've worn the standard TS clothes and boots."

She'd hoped Mohammad's answer would've pointed clearly in Cullen's direction. But unless Cullen wore Sturdy Steer boots when he was off duty, or he put them on to throw suspicion on someone from Ridgeway, the boot print she'd found didn't seem to belong to him. Which led her to a more delicate question.

"Um, Mo," she said. "Do you know Simone Springer?"

He raised his eyebrows in surprise. "Simone? Of course, I know her. She's on our maintenance staff. Hardworking. And then she has such an unusual background. You know she's got experience as a circus performer—it makes her handy with all kinds of equipment."

"Does she wear Sturdy Steer boots?"

"Of course. We all wear Sturdy Steer, either shoes or boots." He grabbed one of his ankles and raised his sneaker, revealing the ox signet on the underside. "See?" Dropping his foot back to the carpeting, he let out a full, warm laugh. "Alice, you and your questions…"

Already uncomfortable asking questions about Simone, she appreciated he left it at that. She didn't want the clues to point to her. But Mohammad's answers only confirmed her suspicions, which was that the boot print belonged to her.

They finished their coffees. Mohammad had a meeting, so they said their goodbyes.

As Alice and Ona emerged from the Ridgeway Cleaning building, Alice was deep in thought. Mohammad had confirmed that Cullen equaled trouble. But he hadn't helped her get any closer to proving that Simone wasn't the killer.

"Alice," Ona muttered.

Alice looked up. It was as if her thoughts had conjured an apparition. There she was, striding across the parking lot, with a frown on her face: Simone. She was wearing the light-blue Ridgeway Cleaning jacket, cargo pants, and Sturdy Steer boots.

"You," she said as she came closer.

"Simone—" Alice said.

"You ratted me out to the state police, and now they think I killed Edna."

"I didn't mean to—"

"You think you're clever, just like your mom thought she was. Stay away from me."

She pushed past Alice, shoving her aside. Then vanished into the Ridgeway Cleaning building.

Alice stared at the doors closing behind her. That line

about her mom had cut her deep inside. Her mom, who Becca had once told her solved mysteries in town, was an inspiration. She was the reason Alice had first mustered the courage to investigate Vince Malone's death, the so-called "accident" that had happened when she first came back to Blithedale. And at every step of the way since—as she settled into a new life in Blithedale, as she opened the bookstore, as she looked into the deaths of Dorothy Bowers, and Stewart Conway, and Wade Ridgeway—her mom had been by her side. These days, she felt closer than ever to her mom. Twenty years had passed since she left this world and Alice still missed her, and always would.

"You okay?" Ona took her hand.

"I feel terrible."

"She's angry. That's normal. It doesn't change the fact that you did the right thing."

Alice sighed. "Did I? I should've waited to call Captain Burlap. I should've gathered more clues. But at least, I guess, I'm doing the right thing now."

CHAPTER 17

The Blithedale Woods whispered in the evening breeze. Light spilled across the parking lot behind the What the Dickens Diner, melting into the darkness among the trees. Colonel Brandon, Marianne Dashwood's lover in *Sense and Sensibility*, or rather the Pemberley Inn's mannequin carrying that name, stood facing a big tree. His back was turned to them. In the gloom, Alice could almost imagine he was a real person, and she shuddered. It wasn't just the cool breeze that made her wrap her arms around herself.

"Try again," Becca said.

"Here goes," Ona said and raised a knitting needle.

She threw it. It flew through the air and, with a thunk, burrowed into the tree bark. She'd missed Colonel Brandon again. She'd thrown three so far, each going wide of the target on Brandon's back—a precise point they'd estimated that the needle would need to enter to pierce the heart. They'd drawn a heart to represent the target.

Ona reached down and grabbed another knitting needle from the pile.

Somehow she'd procured stainless steel knitting needles that were sharpened to a deadly point. When asked how she'd found them, she'd simply grinned and said, "The internet—there's nothing you can't buy." Which made Alice imagine thousands of money-hungry people creating murder weapons on demand...yet another reason to shudder.

Ona took aim and threw. This time, the knitting needle struck the mannequin, driving deep into his soft back. But it was a hand's breadth too far to the right of the heart.

"No bull's eye," Ona said, stooping to get another needle, "but closer."

"You're getting better," Alice said.

Becca nodded. "Still, you'd have to be exceptionally skilled to hit that bull's eye."

"So the killer must've practiced this for hours."

"More likely weeks or months," Ona said. "Think of how much force you'd have to use, and how accurate you'd have to be. This is my sixth attempt. The killer threw just once."

While Ona concentrated on her throw, Becca said, "What about a movie club?"

"A movie club?" Alice said. "What are you talking about?"

"Well, Trudy said she didn't have time to do a book club right now. But you can watch a movie in one evening and then talk about it."

Alice sighed. Becca was still trying to include Trudy in social events. Despite being driven by guilt, the sentiment was nice. Alice felt torn between loving Becca for her concern and wanting to steer clear of Trudy. If she was honest with herself, Trudy bothered her. She was too blunt. The idea of spending evenings with her, listening to her bludgeon every movie to death? No, thank you.

She could hear her now: *Why did the heroine do that? That makes no sense.* And: *I bet that character will die—isn't it obvious what's going to happen?* And: *I read about this one—the main character leaves the town at the end.*

Alice hated watching movies with people who spoiled endings or constantly criticized everything. It was a movie. You're supposed to suspend disbelief. Just be quiet and enjoy it.

"Maybe Trudy's fine, and doesn't need a movie club or other activity," she suggested to Becca. "She's got her law firm, after all, which keeps her busy. And it's not like she doesn't seek out other people. She came to the bookstore today, and Ona and I talked to her."

"But she's alone," Becca said.

"Alone doesn't mean lonely."

"I know. I just want to do right by her."

Alice understood. After all, she felt the same way about Simone. She wanted to do right by her, too. She'd made a mess of the situation, but she was sure that she could fix things—she'd find concrete proof that Simone had nothing to do with the murder.

She watched Ona throw another sharpened knitting needle. Thunk. It hit the tree again. But Ona was undeterred. In fact, she seemed to enjoy the activity.

"This is fun," she said, confirming Alice's suspicion.

"Don't get too good at it, or Captain Burlap will want to question you."

Ona threw another needle, and it flew past the tree and into the darkness.

"Ha! No risk of that happening."

Ona got another knitting needle and prepared to throw it. Alice's thoughts returned to Simone. She thought of the tragedy of her big sister's death—and, further back in time, the scandal that forced her family to leave Blithedale. Which brought her back to the burglaries.

She glanced at Becca.

"Becca, what do you know about Jenny Springer?"

"Only what others know."

Becca looked away, taking an interest in the dark woods. She was a lousy liar, especially around Alice and Ona. But why did she feel the need to be so evasive about the Springers? What was she hiding?

"Becca," Alice said more firmly. "Come on. Talk to me."

"It was a long time ago, and there was a lot of gossip. I don't want to dig up old wounds."

"Edna may have died because of old wounds. What really happened?"

Becca let out a long sigh and turned to face Alice. Her eyes were heavy with sadness—and something else: concern.

Concern, Alice wondered, *for me? Why in the world would she worry about me?*

"The burglaries," Alice prompted Becca.

"Yes, the burglaries."

"And Jenny Springer."

"When it began," Becca said, "nobody thought it would prove to be a serial burglar…"

Becca told the story. About 20 years ago, Blithedale had experienced a spate of burglaries. It began small. But as more and more businesses reported theft, the old chief of police, James Sapling, Jimbo's dad, became determined to catch the culprit.

"Back then, Blithedale was the kind of place where people didn't bother to lock their cars or even their front doors. The burglar didn't have to contend with security cameras or safes. My grandmother's diner, where I worked, was no different. In fact, my grandmother had gathered all her earnings from that week to take it to the bank in Tilbury Town, then got busy serving customers and left the task for the next morning. The burglar took it all."

"No."

"Yes, all of it. My grandma was barely making a profit on the diner. Losing that much cash nearly ruined her."

Becca got a faraway look in her eyes, as if gazing back in time. But then her attention fell back onto Alice, and that sadness came back, and for a moment Alice wondered whether her wariness would return.

But Becca seemed to gather courage and continue.

She said, "Chief Sapling tried everything, but the burglar always seemed one step ahead of him. Until the burglar struck again—and struck out. You can probably guess which business got hit next."

"The Yarn Shoppe."

Becca nodded. "Edna kept her cash in the register overnight sometimes, choosing to wait until the end of the week to take the money to Tilbury Town to deposit it in the bank."

"The burglar got a lot."

"The cash register was full. But someone saw the burglar outside the Yarn Shoppe that night. And that someone—"

Becca stopped herself.

Alice said, "What aren't you telling me?"

"Leave it alone, Alice. Please."

A memory floated to the surface of her mind, something Becca said long ago when they first met: "I suspect you're a lot like your mom, and she always figured out how to solve problems." Becca also told her that her mom had helped the diner once, when—

"You're talking about my mom," she said, "aren't you?"

Becca sighed, her shoulders slumping. "I didn't want to get your mom mixed up in this."

"But you're saying she is mixed up in this."

Becca nodded. "Your mom was the one who spotted Jenny outside the Yarn Shoppe. She decided to look into the matter herself and found the stolen money in Jenny's backpack." Becca stumbled over the words, uncharacteristically awkward. "Then Chief Sapling took over, and there was the threat of criminal charges, though Jenny was still a minor. Well, Jenny's dad, our local minister, and her mom, they went from business to business, repaying everyone down to the last dime. They brought Jenny with them, so she could face the victims of her theft and apologize."

"Wow," Alice said. "That must've made an impression on people."

"Yes, but not enough. Rumors floated around that Jenny had only reluctantly apologized and that she insisted she wasn't guilty. The incident tainted the minister. It seemed to poison the family. Not long after that, they moved from Blithedale. I only heard later that Jenny never recovered from the ordeal—the shame seemed to have been too great for her."

Alice considered this new information. "So my mom was the one who accused Jenny Springer of burglary. She solved the mystery Chief Sapling couldn't solve. She—"

"She did what she thought was right."

"And now Simone…"

Becca nodded. "Simone, who believes her sister was innocent, wants someone to blame."

"My mom." Alice swallowed. "She believes my mom…"

The ground tilted beneath her feet. A sickening ball of shame rose in her throat, as she considered what this might mean. If there was any truth to what Simone said, Jenny was innocent—and Alice's mom had accused the wrong person.

She said, "But Mom is dead. And Chief Sapling is gone. So that only leaves…"

Ona threw again. She let out a yelp and fist-pumped the air.

"Look at that."

The knitting needle had hit its mark, piercing the mannequin's heart.

Ona turned, grinning at her friends. Her smile faded.

"Hey," she said. "Why so glum? What did I miss?"

"Edna," Alice said. "Edna was the only one left to blame. Which means—"

Becca nodded. "Which means Simone has a motive."

CHAPTER 18

*a*t Edna's funeral, Alice hung back from the others, standing under an old oak tree.

Since Becca had revealed that her mom was to blame for Jenny Springer being accused of the burglaries, which ultimately ruined her life, she hadn't felt like being around people.

Despite Becca and Ona insisting she join them at the diner in the morning, she'd grabbed a breakfast pie to go from Bonsai & Pie and eaten it at the bookstore. She'd tried to focus on work, but a storm raged inside her. Her mind was a weathervane swinging this way and then that. How could she calmly go about organizing her books? She couldn't.

Even a visit from the cheerful Mr. and Mrs. Oriel couldn't calm her. They left after a few words, sensing, perhaps, that Alice didn't want company. She'd closed the bookstore early to go to the funeral.

Now she was hiding at the back, watching as Edna's coffin descended into the ground, and thinking, *This is a long story, stretching back 20 years. What happened? Did mom really destroy Jenny's life?*

She couldn't help but suspect that history was repeating itself. Just as she'd jumped to conclusions and pointed the finger at Simone, her mom had wrongfully accused Jenny. Or had it been justified?

Mom, she thought, *what did you do?*

She buried her face in her hands. She tried to think it through again. But she reached the same sickening conclusion over and over and over again.

A hand touched her shoulder. Then fingers grazed her hands, and she lowered them. Becca and Ona were standing there.

"We know you'd like to be alone," Becca said. "But we don't need to talk. We'd just like to stand here with you. All right?"

Silently, Alice nodded.

Her friends arranged themselves on either side of her, flanking her shoulders. They were like sentinels, personal guards, there to protect and defend her. With that thought, a lump, thick and painful, rose in her throat, burning as it went. She choked back the sob.

Who grabbed whose hands first? She couldn't be sure. Maybe she instinctively reached for her friends. Maybe they sought to comfort her. In any case, she found herself clutching Ona's hand on one side and Becca's on the other as tears trickled down her face. The tears were for Jenny and Simone. The tears were for her mom, that infallible ghost, whose spirit had been her only companion for so long, and who might not have been infallible, after all...

She took a deep, shuddering breath.

Through her tears, she watched the minister throw dirt into the grave. There was a sizable crowd. Lillian and Cullen McGlinty stood by themselves, Trudy close by. Jolene and

Hildegarde—one short, the other tall—were joined by Captain Burlap and Beau Bowers. There were others, too: Lorraine, Sandy, Todd Townsend of *The Blithedale Record*, scribbling away on a notepad, and Mayor MacDonald wearing what must be his one suit that wasn't a stark Samuel Clemens white.

After the minister had said his words, the crowd dispersed.

Alice let go of her friends' hands and approached the freshly dug grave. The headstone said,

Edna Lawner

R.I.P.

Happiness is a butterfly…

"I wonder what her epitaph means," Ona said. She dug out her phone, swiped and tapped, and then said, "Huh. I guess Edna was a Lana Del Rey fan. I didn't picture her listening to that kind of music—I had her pegged as the Perry Como type." She kept scrolling. "Oh, wait. Never mind. It's also from a quote by Hawthorne."

"Nathaniel Hawthorne?" Alice asked.

"That's the one. Here's the full quote."

She held up her phone and read:

"Happiness is a butterfly, which, when pursued, is always just beyond your grasp, but which, if you will sit down quietly, may alight upon you."

She lowered her phone. "Wow. That's either very pretty or just plain sad."

"Maybe happiness was always just out of reach for Edna," Becca suggested.

"Maybe…" Alice said, distracted by a lone figure in the distance.

A woman in a dark coat was walking down one of the

cemetery's gravel paths. Everyone else had headed toward the exit. But she was moving in the opposite direction.

"I'll be right back," Alice said.

"You sure?" Becca said. "Happy to join you."

"Yes, more than happy," Ona said.

Alice gave Becca a quick hug and then Ona.

"I'm all right. I promise."

Alice left Becca and Ona by Edna's grave. Down the gravel path and beyond a cypress tree, she found the woman standing by a headstone. She hung her head, seemingly lost in thought or prayer.

Her coat was threadbare. Its original black had lost its luster, while a patch near the hem had held on to its dark dye, making the wear and tear even more visible.

"Jolene?"

Jolene looked up. Behind her wire-rim glasses, her eyes were bloodshot. She stared at Alice for a moment, then looked down again. Fresh flowers brightened the grave.

"It would've broken his heart to see us like this," Jolene said. "One dead and two not talking to each other."

She gestured at the headstone. It said,

Fred Burr
Beloved by all, resting in peace

"Of course, before he died, it wasn't any better." She shook her head. "He lived in a fantasy world. We ought to all be friends, he thought. He couldn't see that what he'd done—left Lillian and then Edna—would drive a wedge between us. But even so, maybe I believed him a little. Maybe I hoped..."

Alice moved closer, coming to her side.

"You joined the knitting club to rekindle your friendship with Edna."

Jolene nodded. "I thought after Fred died, the old

animosities would disappear. There was no reason for us to be rivals any more. But I was mistaken."

"They never hated Fred? Why?"

"Fred made them feel special. Even after he left them. He would visit Lillian. She was married to his best friend, after all, so it wasn't strange that he should hang out at their home. And after divorcing Edna, he kept blaming himself for the break-up. He made sure she was comfortable."

"Alimony?"

"There was alimony, yes. But he gave her more." Jolene paused, took a breath, let it out, and said, "Much more."

Alice waited. She sensed Jolene engaged in an internal debate with herself, desperately wanting to talk to someone. Widowhood could throw people into sudden, shocking loneliness, and for Jolene it would be extra hard, because she had no one to confide in. Alice remained quiet, ready to listen.

Finally, Jolene said, "Fred was an electrician, and he did very well for himself. Mind you, he wasn't rich, just comfortable. *We* were comfortable. But when Fred died, I learned that he'd left part of the inheritance to Edna."

"Wait," Alice said, taken aback. "You mean he left Edna money? How much?"

"Oh, Fred was generous."

"The lion's share?"

"Not quite so much," Jolene said in a small voice. "But close."

"And you didn't contest it?"

Jolene looked down at her feet. "I didn't think it would be the right thing to do."

Alice thought of Edna's modest clothing. Modest? Heck, she wore clothes that had been mended many times over. Fred must've left her with too little to live comfortably on. How had it felt to Jolene to know that Edna, who had received a chunk of Fred's inheritance, wouldn't even talk to her?

"What about Lillian?"

"Fred left her some personal things, but no money. He felt Bill, her husband, had plenty." Jolene tugged at her worn-out coat, pulling it against her as if she were cold. "Bill left Lillian a fortune. She has all the money she could ever dream of."

Alice studied Jolene: her red-eyed grief, her gray-mouse demeanor—could this be an act, a mask concealing a cold-blooded killer? It was hard to imagine. But then the least likely suspect sometimes turned out to be the killer, at least in the mystery novels Alice liked to read.

On the other hand, Jolene was an outsider, someone who, though she knew the others involved, had been pushed aside. It might've forced her to play the role of observer. Maybe she'd seen something.

"Jolene," Alice said. "Did you see or hear anything strange on Sunday night?"

"When Edna was…?"

Alice nodded.

Jolene stared into the middle distance, apparently trying to recall the events of that night.

"I arrived late," she said. "Because of a meeting with my insurance agent. Someone smashed a window, climbed in, and stole God-knows-what. So I got there a little late, and outside the store, I bumped into Lillian."

"She came alone? Or was she with her son?"

"Cullen?" Jolene shook her head. "No, it was her chauffeur who dropped her off. I saw him drive away."

"Then you went inside."

Jolene described the rest of the evening, but her observations simply matched what Alice already knew.

Alice tried to get her to dig deeper. "Did you see anyone

CHAPTER 19

A beam of light stretched across a chair and then the low table. Objects came into view—the carafe of shimmering water with squat glasses crowding below, and the cups, too, huddling under towering thermoses—everything darkening again as the beam crept over another chair. The light shot past the chair and climbed the shelves full of yarn, their colors dimmed in the dark.

"One second," Alice said. "Let me turn my flashlight on, too."

"Weird that the lights don't work again," Ona said. "On Sunday night, when the cops arrived, the first thing they did was turn on the lights again."

Becca moved her flashlight across the Yarn Shoppe again. "Maybe a fuse went."

"We'll have to check the circuit breakers," Ona said.

Alice's phone flashlight joined Becca's. Ona dug out her phone and cast light across the room, too. With three flashlights on, the shadows retreated to the corners.

The setup looked the same as Alice remembered: eight simple chairs arranged neatly in a circle, with the ninth,

Edna's antique, placed with its back to the window. The window was closed and latched—no doubt Captain Burlap's precaution to keep intruders out. But the old lock on the door had been easy to break open.

Staring at Edna's chair and then the window, Alice had a rather disappointing thought.

"What if Edna's chair was the one that made the scraping sound? What if that was what Jolene heard?"

"You mean when Edna was stabbed, and she fell forward?" Ona asked. "Have you tried lifting this chair? It's mighty heavy."

"You're right. Also, I could be mistaken, but it doesn't look like it's been moved. Look where it's placed in relation to Lillian's chair." She shone her flashlight onto the chair to the right of Edna's. Then she brought the chair to the left into the spotlight. "This one looks like it's been moved forward."

Becca shone a light on the chair, too. "Hildegarde was sitting there, wasn't she?"

They examined each chair in the circle, methodically checking them. Edna had carefully arranged the circle of chairs for the knitting club. But, of course, people would shift and move theirs a little when they sat. Beau's was an inch back. Hildegarde's was two inches forward and slightly askew.

Becca said, "Remember that Hildegarde arrived late. Her chair was added to the circle, and it meant everyone had to shift a little. Which may explain why hers isn't perfectly lined up. It doesn't mean she moved it. Besides, when people get up from a chair, they push it back, not forward."

Alice sighed. "And even if the killer shifted their chair, making the sound that Jolene heard, the culprit might've stabbed Edna, then returned to their seat and pushed it forward."

Ona shone her light on Beau's chair. "Beau's is the one furthest back."

"You think Beau killed Edna?"

Ona laughed. "We all know Beau isn't a killer—we've been through all that already."

Alice agreed. When Beau's sister had died, she'd thought he, the wayward brother, had the best motive for the murder, but it had turned out to be an absurd idea—Beau wouldn't hurt a fly. She didn't know the women who'd joined the knitting circle well enough, though. Any one of them could be a killer.

"I don't think these chairs are going to tell us anything else," Alice said.

"Should we look out back?" Ona said.

They moved across the shop and around the counter, careful not to disturb the crime scene. Forensics had come and gone. Captain Burlap might not even need to come back to the Yarn Shoppe. But the less they messed with potential evidence, the better—and besides, they didn't want to leave too much evidence of their break-in.

Too late for that, Alice thought. *You can't fix that lock on the door after breaking it open.*

The door behind the counter was shut. Alice buried her hand in her sleeve so she wouldn't leave fingerprints on the handle, and opened the door.

The back room was small. Their flashlight beams cut across bookshelves, a desk, and another door that opened to a closet-sized restroom.

"Bingo," Ona said, shining a light on a square object jutting out of the wall. "The breaker box."

She crossed the room and pried open the box.

"Hey, Alice, Becca, shine a light on this, will you?"

Alice and Becca joined her and aimed their flashlights at the box so Ona could see what she was doing.

"Hmm…interesting," she said. "The breakers are fine. It doesn't look like there was a power outage. But there's some kind of device installed alongside the circuits…looks like…" She leaned closer and fiddled with a panel that had a small LCD display and several buttons. "It's a timer. Someone installed a timer to cut the power every night. It doesn't flip the circuit breakers. So if there were an electrical failure, like an overload or short circuit, the breakers would still shut off to protect the system. Usually people install these timers directly on light switches, but an electrician must've decided this was more efficient."

"Fred Burr, Edna's ex," Alice said. "He was an electrician."

"Makes sense," Ona said. "Anyway, all we have to do is press this and—"

Light bloomed in the back room.

Ona grinned. "Let there be light."

They shut off their flashlights, which they no longer needed to see. And as Alice pocketed her phone, she said, "So this explains why the lights cut out."

"Did Edna forget she had a timer on?" Becca said.

"More likely, the killer snuck back here and changed the time."

"Which suggests the killer knew the shop, even this back room."

Alice gestured around at the small space, crammed with bookshelves and a desk with a vintage, avocado-green Remington typewriter. Other items competed with the type-writer for space on the desktop: stacks of books, a coffee mug full of pens and pencils, and an old newspaper, folded in half.

And something else, too: a stack of postcards.

Alice stepped over to the desk. She picked up a postcard —one of many on a stack, all of them identical, generic tourist postcards—and she flipped it over. It was blank. But one was jammed into the typewriter. She inched the postcard out of the typewriter's roller and read the back: "Vanity working on a weak head produces every sort of mischief."

"Becca, when did you receive that last poison-pen postcard?"

"Oh, it's about a week ago now. They don't seem to be coming anymore."

"There's a simple reason for that." She showed her the postcard. "The poison-pen writer is dead."

CHAPTER 20

The next morning, Alice had arranged to meet Simone at the What the Dickens Diner. She could barely contain her excitement, tapping her foot as she waited. The many cups of coffee she'd already drunk didn't help, either.

After leaving the Yarn Shoppe the night before, she and Becca and Ona had gathered at the Pemberley Inn to put the pieces together. They'd stayed up till 3 am talking.

They might not know who the killer was, but what mattered was this: they had a solid theory of why Edna was killed—and it showed that Simone couldn't be the murderer.

Simone pushed through the door to the diner, spotted Alice, and made a beeline for the booth.

"I got us both coffee," Alice said as Simone slipped onto the leatherette seat opposite her. "Thanks for coming to Blithedale to meet."

"My shift starts this afternoon." Simone spoke dispassionately. "Anyway, I had to meet with Trudy for legal advice. I'm hiring her to help me, since the police may arrest me at any moment."

"They won't."

"You sound confident." The look she gave Alice was cold as she sipped her coffee. "Your mom was confident, too, when she pointed the finger at my sister."

The words hit Alice like a slap to the face.

"I'm sorry," she said, her voice reduced to a whisper. "My mom must've done her best, what she thought was right, and she—"

"Your mom," Simone said with an iciness bordering on hatred, "is not someone I want to talk about. Now tell me why I'm here."

Alice took a deep, shuddering breath.

This isn't about me, she told herself. *Or Mom. It's about Simone, and Edna's murder. It's about doing the right thing.*

"I know you didn't kill Edna."

"Congratulations. You might be the only one."

"Edna was writing poison-pen letters to people. Postcards, actually. She must've rankled the wrong person. The killer, I think, came to silence her. The murder has nothing to do with you and your sister."

"Captain Burlap believes I came to the shop that night for revenge."

"But that's only a theory," Alice insisted, "it assumes—"

"That I was there? For God's sake, Alice, I was there. You saw me at the window. You chased me. How blind are you?"

Another slap across the face. "No…"

"Yes. You were right that I left my boot prints outside. Plus, someone else saw me and reported it to the police. I can't deny it. I crept up to that window." She shook her head. "But I didn't kill Edna."

"I know you didn't. You couldn't have. The killer arranged for the lights to go out at the Yarn Shoppe. It was someone on the inside, not standing outside."

"Unless," Simone said, "that someone broke into the Yarn Shoppe days in advance."

"But you didn't." Alice swallowed. "Did you?"

"Captain Burlap found my fingerprints."

"Why?"

"Days before her murder, I confronted Edna. She said she'd changed her mind. She believed my sister was innocent. I got the feeling she knew something, but she wouldn't —or couldn't—tell me. Maybe she even had evidence. I broke into the shop to see if I could find something. So, yeah, I could've fiddled with the lights."

"But even if you could've tampered with the timer for the lights, you were standing outside the window. You couldn't have thrown a knitting needle and killed Edna in one go. Me and my friends have tested what it would take to throw a sharpened knitting needle at that distance, and it would take incredible precision and skill to succeed."

"Like a professional knife thrower?"

Alice wondered whether Simone was joking, but there was no joy in her voice, and her face showed no signs of humor. In fact, she looked bitterly serious.

"Uh," Alice said, "I guess so."

"After my sister ran away from home, I couldn't make school work for me. Focusing was hard. I liked sports and theater, but forget about going to college, like my parents wanted me to. I went to Florida and got a job at a hardware store and, in my spare time, attended circus school."

"Circus school?" Alice remembered Mohammad mentioning something about it. At the time, she'd barely registered the detail. Now, its importance hit her like a freight train. "And you studied to be a—a—"

"A trapeze artist. An acrobat. And a knife thrower." Simone smiled. It was a bitter smile. "I was the best at knife throwing, as Captain Burlap has discovered from talking to my instructors and former colleagues. I had such a knack for it I got a job teaching at the school. Then I worked at a circus for a while. You want to know what my most popular routine was?"

Alice wanted to nod, but her head was spinning and her neck had gone rigid.

Simone went on: "I played an old woman who was attacked by demons, and I fought them off with nothing but my knitting needles. There were two acrobats dressed as demons, and I had two knitting needles. I threw them, one after the other. And hit each demon right in their well-padded heart, never missing once." She pushed aside her coffee and got to her feet. "So, you see, Burlap has a solid case against me."

Alice, gazing up at Simone, felt so dizzy she thought she'd be sick.

"But you didn't kill Edna," she said, "did you?"

Simone glared at her. "You'll believe what you want to believe. It doesn't matter what I say."

She spun around and strode away, leaving Alice stunned.

CHAPTER 21

a breeze shook the leaves overheard. The Sunday morning sun filtered through the canopy, dappling the hiking trail with shadows. Somewhere in the distance, a woodpecker rat-tat-tatted the bark of a tree.

Alice dragged her feet, staring at the ground as she trudged forward. She'd spent the rest of Saturday in a deep, dark place, wondering whether her misguided confidence had been arrogance…and whether she'd inherited that arrogance from her mom.

"Come on," Ona said, grabbing her hand and tugging her forward. "Simone hasn't killed every last ounce of optimism in you, has she?"

"She's right. I didn't have enough information, and I jumped to conclusions. I was overly confident."

Like my mom…?

Her mom might have unjustly accused Jenny Springer, ruining her life.

And ruining Simone's, too.

Ona kept tugging her up the hiking trail.

"Simone is angry, and she has a right to be. But that doesn't make her conclusions right."

"But everything she said—"

"Yes, yes." Ona waved a hand dismissively. "Everything she said fits with what Captain Burlap believes—or wants to believe. But he doesn't have a shred of concrete evidence. Simone says she didn't murder Edna, and you believe her, don't you?"

"I do," Alice said. "I just know it in my heart."

"Well, that's good enough for me. But it won't stand up in the court of law. So, come on, let's see if we can solve the mystery of the scraping chair."

The hiking trail curved and up ahead in a clearing stood Hildegarde's cabin. They went to the door and knocked. A moment passed, then it opened.

"Yes?" Hildegarde said, a frown on her face.

"We have another question," Ona said, and nudged Alice. "Don't we, Alice?"

"I don't have to answer your questions."

"No," Ona said, "you don't. But don't you think Edna would want you to?"

Hildegarde crossed her arms. "You didn't know Edna."

Ona said, "We know she was sending poison-pen post-cards to people in Blithedale—anonymous postcards with literary quotes intended to insult or upset people."

Hildegarde grimaced. Then she stepped aside.

"You'd better come inside."

This time, she asked them to sit at her table and she put a kettle on a gas burner. After making them all tea, she sat down with her own steaming mug.

She sighed.

"I guessed it was Edna sending the cards. It was like her to be clever about it. If the postcards had simply contained insults or threats, I would've looked elsewhere for a culprit.

But Edna was a big fan of aphorisms and clever quips. She loved Oscar Wilde."

Alice, despite the cloud that hung over her, couldn't help but be interested in this revelation. She leaned forward and asked, "Do you know why she did it?"

"She was angry," Hildegarde said. "She felt abandoned— first by her husband, then by her friends, and over time, she felt, by the whole town. People she'd grown up with or lived with for many years no longer dropped by her shop. If it hadn't been for Fred's bequest, she would've gone out of business."

Alice thought back to who had received the postcards. What Hildegarde said made sense. Becca, Lorraine, and Beau had received postcards, so had other long-time Blithedalers, whereas newcomers, like herself, Ona, Andrea, and Esther, hadn't been targeted.

Alice said, "Did she send you cards?"

Hildegarde looked offended. "Of course she didn't. We were friends. I often came to see her at the Yarn Shoppe. In fact, she was one of the few reasons I came down to town." She shook her head. "I told her to stop sending the cards. 'Let every man be swift to hear, slow to speak, slow to wrath: for the wrath of man worketh not the righteousness of God.' But she was stubborn. She told me she would do things 'her way.'"

"What happened the night she was murdered? Why did you show up? Did she ask you to come?"

Hildegarde looked away, then glanced back at Alice.

"She asked me to come, yes. So I came."

"Why?"

"She trusted me."

"Which means?"

Hildegarde took a sip of her tea, but said nothing.

Alice said, "Did Edna believe her life was in danger? Did

you join the knitting club to keep an eye on the crowd?" Hildegarde's face remained still, impassive, but Alice sensed she'd struck a nerve. "Why was Edna's life in danger? Because of the postcards?"

"Yes," Hildegarde said.

"Who wanted to kill her?"

Hildegarde shook her head. "I don't know—" Slowly, she got to her feet. "—yet. That's all I can tell you."

Alice and Ona looked at each other. Ona shrugged. They rose from their seats, thanking Hildegarde for the tea. But on the way out, Alice asked another question:

"The night of the murder, I heard a chair scraping. Did you hear it, too?"

"I did," Hildegarde said. "It was my chair."

"You got up?"

She shook her head. Her eyes narrowed as she studied Alice and Ona, her distrust visible in the deepening of her crow's feet. Did she think there was a possibility that one of them could've murdered Edna?

"I moved my chair a little," she said, finally, "because someone bumped me. Someone passed behind me."

Alice's heart did a little flip. "Who? Who was it?"

Hildegarde shook her head, still looking at the two of them. Her caution seemed to ease a little. But she hesitated a little longer. Then she said, "I don't know for certain."

"Do you have a guess?"

"I prefer not to. Guessing before knowing can lead to disaster."

Alice nodded, agreeing. Guessing before knowing might have led her mom to cause a disaster. She wouldn't blame Hildegarde for avoiding that mistake.

They said their goodbyes and headed off down the North Trail again. Ona wondered about what else Hildegarde knew. Together, on the hike back down to town, they speculated about how much Captain Burlap had learned—and how much Hildegarde would withhold, even from the law.

They passed through stunning scenery. Giant trees reaching for the sky. Moss-covered rocks. Birds scampering in the underbrush and then, hearing them approach, fluttering into the canopy.

Alice was just suggesting that Hildegarde believed she answered to a higher law and might never stoop to tell them what she knew when they neared the end of the hiking trail. Ona put out a hand out to stop Alice.

"What?"

"Look—down by the Yarn Shoppe."

A man was moving around the building, creeping along as if he were looking for a way inside, or he'd been snooping along the back. As soon as he looked up, Alice recognized him.

"Cullen McGlinty."

He saw them then, too. His face clenched in an angry frown. But instead of striding up to them, as she'd expect him to, he ducked around the corner of the house and vanished.

Alice and Ona hurried down the trail.

But by the time they reached the Yarn Shoppe, Alice heard the revving of a car engine. She and Ona ran down to Main Street. Just in time to watch Cullen burn rubber and speed away.

They watched the car vanish in the distance.

Ona said, "I'm going to go out on a limb and guess he was up to no good."

"I won't argue with that," Alice said. "The question is, what kind of no good?"

CHAPTER 22

On Monday morning, Alice and Ona got up early to meet Becca at the diner and talk through the case. Becca was unlocking the door to the diner when they got there.

"Good morning," she said.

"It is a good morning," Alice said.

The sun was rising over the Blithedale Woods. The air was crisp and cool and clear, a freshness that made Alice feel as if her lungs were filling—truly filling—for the first time.

She'd slept deeply and woken with a renewed sense of purpose.

Ona's insistence on following up with Hildegarde had worked on two levels: first, Alice had learned something new and, second, it had dispelled some of the dark clouds hanging over her. Occasionally, the reminder of what her mom might have done to Jenny and Simone intruded, but she pushed it away.

Later, she told it. *I'll deal with you later.*

"So," Becca said, opening the door, "who wants coffee? Oh, hold on. My phone's ringing."

She dug out her phone.

"Oh, hi, Susan. Hold on, what's—"

Becca broke off. Her eyes widened.

"Are you all right? Don't move, and don't do anything you'll regret. We'll be right there."

She hung up and shoved her phone in her pocket.

"Ladies," she said. "Saddle up. Susan needs our help. She's caught Cullen harassing her neighbor."

"What neighbor?" Alice asked.

"Jolene. She lives next to Susan."

Becca shepherded them out of the door and locked it. Then gestured toward the parking lot, telling them to pile into her car. They typically traveled in Ona's pickup truck for its convenience, but since Alice and Ona had walked from the Pemberley Inn, jumping into Becca's car would be faster.

It was a candy apple red 1966 Ford Thunderbird convertible, the same model as the one Thelma and Louise drove in Becca's favorite movie. The top was down.

As Becca got behind the wheel, Ona called shotgun. Alice crammed her legs into the backseat and held on to the back of Ona's seat.

"Here we go, ladies."

Becca tore out of the parking lot, the tires screeching as she swung onto Main Street and hit the accelerator. Alice flew back in her seat. Ona let out a loud whoop.

The cool wind made Alice's eyes water. They flew past the dirt lot where Townsend Development had once stood. Becca swung the wheel to the right, and they flew past the boarded-up Darn Good Diner, and then the houses grew sparser, the trees more dense.

By the time they reached the neighborhood of modest ranch-style homes where Susan lived, Alice's face prickled with the constant onslaught of hard wind. It was a relief to climb out of the uncomfortable backseat.

But she quickly forgot her aching back.

Susan, waitress at the What the Dickens Diner, stood a few paces away holding a baseball bat. Cullen McGlinty held a switchblade.

Susan, glancing over her shoulder at her friends, said, "Glad you came. This creep won't leave."

"Take another step," Cullen said, "and I'll be forced to defend myself."

Susan snorted. "Defend yourself. Don't be ridiculous. You were trying to force your way into Jolene's home."

"Your word against mine."

"What do you say we call Sheriff Cutter or the state police and see if they agree?"

Cullen said nothing. With a sour glare, he eyed Alice, Becca, and Ona, who had positioned themselves at Susan's sides. They outnumbered him. His skill with a switchblade—and willingness to use it—no doubt gave him an advantage, but Alice guessed he was the kind of man who was used to intimidating lone women, not brazen enough to take on four. She hoped she was right.

"Go," Becca said. "Leave now."

"I didn't break any laws," he said.

Ona said, "You're here to intimidate Jolene. I'd say the police won't be happy about that. Or about that switchblade."

"I came to ask Mrs. Burr a few questions."

"Yeah, right. Why would you want to talk to Jolene?"

His glare gradually transformed into a smirk. He flipped his switchblade, and with a snick-snick, it folded up. He shoved it into a pocket, then reached inside his jacket.

"Whoa there, buddy," Susan said, raising her bat.

"Wallet," he said. "Not a gun."

He extracted a wallet, and with the same deft motion he'd folded the switchblade, he flicked it open, revealing a badge.

Alice drew in a sharp breath of air.

A badge?

"Where did you get that," Ona said, "at a costume store?"

"If you come closer, you can decide for yourself."

"No, thank you."

He shrugged and flipped his wallet closed. "Suit yourself. It says I'm a licensed private investigator. I was moonlighting as a P.I. while I worked security—but now it's my main gig."

Ona frowned and glanced at Alice. Alice was as puzzled as Ona looked. Becca shook her head, too, and Susan lowered her bat a little.

Alice said, "If you're a P.I., why are you bothering Jolene?"

Cullen grinned. "Because it's my job. I'm investigating on behalf of my client."

"And who's your client?"

"Lock, Stock, and Barrel Law."

Becca gasped. "Trudy hired you? I don't believe it."

"Believe it." He glanced back at the house and shrugged. "I'll come back later to talk to Mrs. Burr. Eventually, she'll tell me what I need to know."

He headed their way, charting a direct course toward them. Susan raised the bat again. Unfazed by the threat, Cullen kept coming and—losing his little game of chicken—they all instinctively stepped aside, which made him smirk again.

He reached a car parked by the curb. It was the same car Alice and Ona had seen him drive away from the Yarn Shoppe. He walked around it and yanked open the driver's door. Then leaned against the roof.

"I'm investigating the Edna Lawner murder. So I'll look forward to talking to you—" He pointed his index finger at Becca and raised his thumb, like the cocked trigger of a pistol, and pretended to fire, moving from her to Ona and then to Alice. "—and you, and you."

Then he ducked into the car. The car's engine growled, and it shot forward, tearing down the street and turning and then disappearing.

Alice stood stunned by the curb.

"Cullen McGlinty," Ona said, incredulous, "a private investigator?"

Behind them, a door cracked open and Alice turned to see Jolene peering out with big, terrified eyes.

"Is he gone?"

CHAPTER 23

*W*hile Becca and Susan returned to the diner to open for the day, Alice and Ona stayed with Jolene to calm her down. Apparently, Cullen had come to the door and demanded to know what she knew about Edna's death. He'd asked questions in a way that insinuated Jolene knew more than she said she did. Then, when she hadn't answered in ways he liked, he'd tried to force his way past her and into her home.

"Bizarre behavior for a private investigator," Alice said.

Ona shrugged. "He's a bizarre guy."

"I'm not so sure. I would've said he was creepy. But bizarre?"

Alice left Ona with Jolene. Maybe the widow would open up to Ona and reveal something new—though Jolene insisted she could barely recall the night of Edna's murder, she was so upset by it.

Alice walked back to the town center. It took a while, but it gave her time to think about what in the world could've possessed Trudy to hire Cullen as a private investigator. By the time she reached the offices of Lock, Stock, and Barrel

Law, she was bursting with questions—and tensing with anger.

She walked through the door. The carpeted floors muffled her steps, but she wouldn't have heard them anyway —her heart was hammering so loudly in her ears.

Trudy was talking to Mayor Townsend near the back.

Alice cut off their conversation. "Is it true you hired Cullen McGlinty as a private investigator?"

Trudy smiled, those big teeth dominating her face. "Sure I did."

The casualness with which she said it took Alice aback.

"And he's investigating Edna's murder? Why? And what were you thinking? First, the man's own mother may be a suspect. Second, he's a bully with a known history of intimidating people and—"

Trudy clamped a hand down on Alice's arm. Her grip was powerful. She smiled at Mayor Townsend and said, "Excuse us for a moment. Alice and I need to discuss this in private."

Then she dragged Alice into her office and shut the door.

She spun around to face Alice, shoving a finger in her face.

"Don't slander me in front of the mayor," she hissed.

"I wasn't—"

"If you smear my reputation, I swear—" She jabbed Alice in the chest with her finger. "—I'll destroy you."

This got Alice angry. "I wasn't smearing your reputation. I was stating the facts, as relayed to me by your henchman, Cullen McGlinty."

"He's not my 'henchman.' He's a legitimate private investigator, and I hired him because he's tough and won't take no for an answer. Yes, he's a bull in a china shop, but Simone's freedom is at stake. We need to build an effective defense for her. Don't you agree?"

"Of course I agree."

Trudy eyed her coldly. "Do you? I have my doubts. You think Simone would be better off if an amateur like yourself investigated? You think that would help us get her off the hook?"

"I—"

Alice was suddenly confused. How had this become about her?

Trudy went on: "I know what your mom did back in the day with the Jenny Springer case. Jenny was innocent. You, of all people, should know how damaging amateur sleuthing can be."

The accusation stunned Alice. Her lungs seemed to have lost all air. No retort came to mind. She could only stand and stare, horrified, at Trudy.

Trudy nodded to herself. "If I had a penny for every time I met a private citizen who thought they knew law and order better than the professionals, I'd be a millionaire by now. You think you're part of the solution, Alice, but you're not."

Trudy stepped past her and opened the door, extending a hand to show that the conversation was over. It was time to leave.

"No, you're not the solution," Trudy said. "You're the problem."

CHAPTER 24

With heavy steps, Alice made her way back to the diner. Her whole body felt stiff. Every time she took a breath, a sharp pain jabbed her, as if a thorn lodged in her chest.

Trudy seemed so convinced, she thought. *Was Jenny really innocent? Did Mom accuse the wrong person? And am I repeating her mistakes?*

As she approached the What the Dickens Diner, she saw a state trooper by a cruiser. Cullen leaned against his own car, arms crossed, talking to the cop. Even if Cullen was reprehensible, he was a licensed private investigator. He belonged. Alice didn't need a clearer image of the truth Trudy had spoken: there were people working for law and order, and she wasn't one of them.

The door to the diner swung open and Captain Burlap emerged with another cop. Who was leading Simone, handcuffed, toward the cruiser. She held her head high, a look of angry defiance on her face. But her jaw muscles twinged, betraying how hard she was trying to control her emotions.

Cullen called out to her. "I've messaged Trudy. She'll meet

you at the police station. She said for you to keep quiet until then. Got it?"

Simone nodded.

The state trooper put a hand on Simone's head and guided her into the back of the cruiser, then shut the door. The cops got in the car and Captain Burlap was about to get into his own vehicle when a tall figure crossed the street and swept in front of him, blocking him.

"Captain Burlap," Hildegarde said with the brook-no-argument authority of an old-fashioned schoolmarm, "let that woman go at once. She's not your killer."

"Oh?" Captain Burlap said. "I'm afraid the evidence suggests she is."

"Evidence." Hildegarde grimaced, showing him how little respect she had for that word. "God knows she is innocent, and you'll be setting yourself against His will by judging this lamb."

Captain Burlap sighed. "God may know. You may even know. But until you can provide me with evidence as strong as what I have now, you'll have to pardon me, ma'm, because I've got a murder investigation to wrap up."

He gave her a nod, stepped past her, and got into his car.

A moment later, he was driving off, catching up to the state troopers.

Cullen laughed, apparently enjoying Hildegarde's failure to stop Burlap.

But Hildegarde, undeterred, said to herself, loud enough for Alice to hear: "If he wants evidence, he can have it. Plenty of it."

And with that, she spun around and strode down the street, heading in the direction, Alice assumed, of the North Trail—and her cabin in the woods.

Alice watched her go. She heard Cullen's car come to life. He revved the engine and did a quick three-point turn and drove off, turning up the road that led into the woods. A small crowd had gathered to gossip, but Alice was busy with her own thoughts.

Simone's innocent, an inner voice accused, *and you got her arrested.*

And even if she's not, then you meddled in a murder investigation just because your "heart" told you she didn't kill Edna.

Either way, you're not the solution...

"I'm the problem..." she muttered to herself.

Becca and Ona came out of the diner and they joined Alice.

"We've got to stop this," Ona said, gazing down Main Street at where the cops had disappeared with Simone.

Alice shook her head. "We shouldn't meddle. Captain Burlap knows what he's doing. He must have a good reason for arresting Simone."

Becca nodded. "Too good a reason, if you ask me."

Despite the voice in her head, Alice couldn't help but ask, "What do you mean?"

"He said they got an anonymous call that led them to revisit the crime scene. In the bushes outside the Yarn Shoppe's window, they found a second knitting needle, sharpened to a deadly point. And he says they pulled a clear fingerprint from it."

"Simone's?"

"Of course."

"But then it must be true..."

Becca gave her a sharp look. "What's got into you? Aren't you listening to me? Someone obviously got Simone to hold that knitting needle, sharpened it, and then planted it. Someone—"

It was as if warm blood suddenly rushed through Alice's veins, bringing her body back to life. A fog lifted from her brain. She straightened up.

"Cullen," she said. "We saw him outside the Yarn Shoppe, sneaking around." She looked around. "Where is he? Where did he go?"

Then she knew.

"Hildegarde. Quick." She grabbed Becca's hand and Ona's hand and squeezed them. "We've got to go. We've got to stop this—before it's too late."

CHAPTER 25

Ona hit the brakes hard and her pickup dug deep into
the soft dirt outside Hildegarde's cabin in the
woods. The abrupt stop threw Alice forward. The seatbelt bit
into her shoulder. But in an instant, she undid it and jumped
out of the car.

Becca slid out of the pickup, too.

Another car was parked outside the cabin. A rust-fringed
Mazda that showed signs of hard use since its birth in the
1990s.

"Cullen's?"

Alice shook her head. "Cullen's car is black. Besides, I
don't think he'd drive a compact car like this."

"Then who—?"

Just then, the door to the cabin opened, and Lillian and
Jolene stepped out.

"Thank goodness," Jolene said. "We were afraid you
were—"

She cut herself off and glanced nervously at Lillian.

"It's all right," Lillian said. "You can say it. My son. We

were afraid you were my son. Where's Hildegarde? Is she with you?"

Alice's heart sank. "We hoped she was here."

Lillian shook her head. "The door was open when we arrived."

Ona strode over to the cabin and looked inside. She nodded. "Empty."

Alice looked over her shoulder—trees all around, but no sign of Hildegarde—then down at the ground. Next to the deep grooves Ona's pickup had made, there were two other sets of tracks. One clearly belonged to Jolene's car (it must be Jolene's—Alice was sure Lillian would never drive a rundown compact), so the other tire tracks must belong to Cullen's.

"He was here," she guessed, "and he took Hildegarde."

"She called us," Jolene said.

Lillian nodded. "I was surprised. Hildegarde using a telephone. I thought she was an incurable Luddite, but there's a payphone at the theater—she called us from there."

"She told us to both get to her cabin immediately," Jolene said, continuing where Lillian had left off. "She called me first, and I told her I'd pick up Lillian."

"Imagine my surprise when I got the call from Hildegarde. A few minutes later, I was waiting outside my gates to hitch a ride with Jolene. I decided I'd rather drive with her than ask my chauffeur. He's wonderful, but whenever I ask him to drive fast, he lectures me on the dangers of traffic and—"

"Lillian," Jolene said, putting a hand on the other woman's arm, gently interrupting her. "We ought to tell them what Hildegarde told us."

"Oh, yes," Lillian said. "Of course. Go ahead, Jolene. You explain."

"Well, Hildegarde called us and told us that Simone was

arrested. She told us she knows we didn't kill Edna. Because she figured out who did it. She wasn't sure at first, but once Cullen came into the picture, she was convinced."

Lillian shook her head. "Cullen."

Alice studied Lillian's face. Despite the years of plastic surgery, emotion marked her features—sadness, but also something else.

"You're afraid of him," Alice said. "You're afraid of your son."

"Of course not. He's my little boy." Lillian looked away, her face hardening. "Deep down, he's a good boy. Only he gets carried away. He aspires to be a success, like his daddy. But the way he gets things done..." She shuddered. "And if Mommy doesn't let him do what he likes to do, then he gets mad. Really mad."

"Did you know he was fired from his job in security for sabotage and for threatening a competitor?"

Lillian shook her head, visibly deflating.

Alice added, "And did you know that he's been hired as a detective for Trudy at Lock, Stock, and Barrel Law? He's working on Edna's murder investigation."

"Oh, no..." Lillian said, her voice barely a whimper.

Jolene wrapped an arm around her old friend to support her.

Becca joined her, giving Lillian comfort. Meanwhile, Ona gestured at Alice to follow her inside. She said, "We've got to find out what Hildegarde knows. But how?"

Alice, stepping inside, scanned the cabin. Drawers in the kitchen had been pulled out. Kitchen utensils lay scattered on the floor. An old chest stood open, sheets and blankets yanked halfway out. Clearly, Cullen had been looking for something. But did he find it?

Then Alice's eyes fell on a part of the room Cullen hadn't bothered to touch: the bookshelf full of Bibles.

Maybe he'd dismissed it as unimportant. But Alice noticed it looked different, somehow, from last time. One book didn't fit.

The spine said, *Kierkegaard: Either/Or.* This work of theological philosophy didn't belong among the Bibles.

"Hildegarde must've guessed she was in danger. She left this for us."

Alice grabbed the book and flipped it open. The inside had been torn out. Instead, it contained a thick wad of folded papers, newspaper clippings, and photographs.

She brought the items to the table and laid them out.

Ona joined her, helping her spread them out so they could make sense of what Hildegarde had collected.

A single sheet of paper that was folded, as if it had been inside an envelope, contained a message in recognizable font —Edna must've typed it on her old Remington.

```
Hildegarde,


Hold on to this report for me. You're
the only person I trust. The real
culprit, who I've invited to our knit-
ting club tomorrow, may try to steal
this. I've already had two break-ins.

See you tomorrow,

Edna
```

Beneath this cover letter was a thicker ream of papers stapled together. The first page had also been typewritten but clearly using a different machine. And longer ago: the edges of the papers had yellowed with age.

It was headed, "Report on serial burglar in Blithedale."

Below that was a date from over 20 years ago, and then a message that made Alice catch her breath:

CHIEF SAPLING,

AS PROMISED, THIS REPORT CONTAINS EVERYTHING I KNOW ABOUT THE BURGLARIES. AS I EXPLAIN, I CAN'T DRAW ANY CONCLUSIONS. I CAN ONLY TELL YOU WHAT I'VE FOUND. I WOULD CONTINUE TO HELP YOU LOOK FOR THE BURGLAR, BUT I'VE GOTTEN SOME BAD NEWS FROM THE DOCTOR. I LEAVE THE INVESTIGATION IN YOUR CAPABLE HANDS.

B. HARTFORD

Alice's hands shook. The text on the page blurred, and she reached up and wiped a tear from her face. Then she turned the page and read the first page of the report. Then the next.

She looked up at Ona, the tears now streaming down her face. "Mom didn't accuse Jenny of theft. She gathered the evidence, but she turned it over to Chief Sapling, and he was the one who jumped to the conclusion that Jenny was guilty."

"Does she say who she thinks did it?"

Alice shook her head. "Only that the damning evidence—the money found in Jenny's backpack—ought to be questioned, because it was so conveniently discovered after an anonymous call."

"Sounds suspicious."

"Exactly. And it sounds a lot like Captain Burlap's anonymous caller, who led him to the evidence tying Simone to the murder."

Among the documents was a newspaper clipping about a church bake sale. A strange thing to include, Alice thought, until she saw the photograph. A younger Hildegarde stood alongside Lillian, Jolene, and Edna. But there were two kids as well. Late teens. And someone had circled one of them with a pen. The ink was recent. Hildegarde must've done it.

Becca came through the door.

"Alice, Ona, any progress? Lillian's told me more about Cullen's temper, and it's got me worried. Forget I said that. It's got me terrified. She describes him as a kind of pit bull, trained to bite. We've got to find Hildegarde before it's too late."

"But he could've taken her anywhere," Ona said.

Alice shook her head. "No. Even a pit bull runs back to its master when it's called."

"Master? What master?"

Alice pointed to the newspaper clipping. The caption said, "Jenny Springer and Gertrude Lockstock."

Hildegarde had circled Trudy's face and that big, toothy grin.

CHAPTER 26

The sign on the door of Lock, Stock, and Barrel Law said, "Closed." The blinds were down. But Lillian and Jolene knocked anyway, then settled down on the bench outside with their knitting, a tote bag leaning against Lillian's side.

No one came to the door.

"This'll never work," Ona said.

"Keep watching," Alice said.

They were hiding behind Ona's pickup truck across the street. Alice was inclined to agree with Ona. Her heart was racing. Every beat seemed one more second wasted—one more step toward Hildegarde's death.

Ona tapped her fingers against the edge of the flatbed.

"At least Lillian and Jolene look calm."

They did. The two friends—obviously no longer enemies —sat side-by-side on the bench, calmly engaged in their knitting.

"Should we tell them to knock again?" Ona said.

Alice shook her head. "We'll just draw attention to

ourselves. My gut tells me Cullen and Trudy will be very alert to what's going on outside."

Sure enough, the blinds shook, as if someone had shifted them aside to take a peek. Then the door opened and Cullen's head appeared.

Even at a distance, Alice heard him clearly.

"Mommy," he said. "What's up? What've I told you about interrupting me at work?"

"Oh, sweetheart, I just wanted to ask you something important…"

"It can wait." Cullen began to close the door. But not all the way. He was watching his mom, a frown gathering on his face. He glanced at Jolene. The mousey woman didn't say a thing, simply moved her knitting needles in a steady rhythm.

"All right, what?" he said.

"I found something you might need for your work," Lillian said, her eyes on her knitting, as if they were having a completely innocuous conversation—about the weather or what to eat for dinner. "Hildegarde left me some documents she said were important. But you know me, sweetie, I don't know about these things…"

"Documents? What documents?"

He pushed the door open wider.

Lillian shrugged, still focused on her knitting. "Who knows? A report of some kind."

Cullen shot out of the doorway, taking three strides to get to the bench. Jolene didn't stop what she was doing. She didn't even look up.

He thrust out a hand. "Gimme."

Lillian paused her knitting and looked up at him. Her voice shook a little, but she didn't flinch as she stared at him.

"No, Cullen," she said.

He clenched his fists and stepped closer, jaw set in a

threatening manner. "Don't make me lose my patience. Give me the documents, *now*."

"You wouldn't hurt me, would you?"

Cullen snorted. "Try me."

Lillian stared at him for another moment, then sighed, apparently giving in to his threat. She set down her knitting to reach for the tote bag next to her. Reaching into the bag, she dug out a stack of papers and waved them at him.

"Is this what you're looking for?"

"Yes!"

Cullen grabbed the papers. Lillian picked up her knitting, while Jolene seemed to struggle with a particularly tricky loop. Her face was set in a determined scowl. She must've solved the problem, because her features smoothed again and she continued the steady click of her needles.

Cullen flipped through the papers. "Are these all the documents? You're sure?"

"This is everything Hildegarde gave me," Lillian said.

"Great." A grin spread across his face. "This is exactly what my boss wants."

He turned to head back inside, but his legs caught on something and he let out a surprisingly high-pitched, "Hey," and then fell face forward. His hands scrambled to save him. The papers went flying. But the extra staples Alice had added held them together, and Lillian, leaping up, caught the bundle.

Cullen cursed loudly. He thrashed his legs, caught in a large loop of yarn.

Jolene laughed, delighted.

"Gotcha!"

In an instant, Becca had crossed the street and crouched down with a big roll of duct tape, which she began weaving around Cullen's legs. He tried to punch her, but Lillian put a stiletto heel on his chest, apparently sharp enough to give him pause.

"I'll teach you a—" he said.

"A lesson?" Lillian pressed her heel down and Cullen winced. "You're not teaching anyone anything. I'll make sure of that."

Alice and Ona moved around the truck and headed straight for the door to the law office. Ona pulled open the door and Alice slipped inside. Ona was right behind her.

Inside, with the blinds down and no lights on, the reception desk and shelves and office plants created deeply shadowed nooks. Alice and Ona crept across the floor, and Alice was glad for how the carpeting muffled her steps.

The door to the office at the back stood open. Alice crept up to the doorway. She took a deep breath and then peeked inside.

Hildegarde sat in a chair, her arms and legs tied. She'd been gagged, too, but she looked as stoic as ever. When she saw Alice, she gave a nod. But it wasn't just a nod of recognition. It was a nod that suggested something else. More like a "look over there" nod.

Alice moved over to the desk.

"Here?" she whispered.

Hildegarde nodded.

Alice opened the desk drawer. For a moment, she had the bizarre notion that she was looking at a drawer full of chopsticks. Metal chopsticks? No. Knitting needles. Then she realized what they were: a whole drawer full of metal knitting needles sharpened to a deadly point.

How simple to take one out, she thought, *and give it to Simone and ask her to assess it as part of a "thorough" investigation, capturing Simone's fingerprint.*

"Ona," she said. "We've got the evidence."

Alice turned back toward Ona. But Ona, standing in the doorway, wasn't alone. Trudy stood next to her. And she was pressing a gun into Ona's side.

"Like mother," Trudy said through gritted teeth, "like daughter."

CHAPTER 27

*T*rudy dug the gun deeper into Ona's side, making Ona flinch.

"I should shoot your friend right now, then get rid of you, too."

"Smart idea," Alice said. "Nobody will wonder why someone is firing a gun on a Monday morning in Blithedale."

"This little gun has a built-in suppressor. People will think they heard a door slam. That's all."

She pushed Ona into the office. Pointing the gun at her, she motioned for her to join Alice, which she did. This put some distance between them and Trudy.

She must want some space, Alice thought. *So she can shoot us without us trying any heroics.*

She needed to distract Trudy. "You thought framing Simone and getting rid of Hildegarde would fix the problem."

"And it would've," Trudy snapped. "If it hadn't been for your meddling."

"Edna wrote a poison-pen postcard to you, didn't she?"

Trudy waved the gun, gesturing at a cork board. One item pegged to the board was a postcard showing scenes from Niagara Falls. Next to it was another card, one showing the Statue of Liberty.

Trudy said, "The first card said, 'There is no honor among thieves.' I ignored it. But the next one made me suspicious. It was from the Bible: 'For there is nothing hidden that will not be disclosed, and nothing concealed that will not be known or brought out into the open.' Did someone know my secret? Did someone know about me and Jenny? If the truth came out now, it would destroy my reputation as a lawyer. I couldn't let that happen."

"Jenny was your friend," Alice said. "You used your friendship to set her up."

"She was a naive girl. It was easy to send her a cryptic, anonymous invitation to meet at night at the Yarn Shoppe. She snuck out that night, and there she was, standing in the dark by the store, waiting for her secret admirer. A mystery man who'd never turn up." Trudy chuckled. "Your mom saw her. And later, when she snooped around Jenny's backpack, I made sure a wad of money was tucked into an inner pocket."

"By why?" Alice said. "Why frame Jenny?"

"Chief Sapling and his little sidekick, your mom, were getting too close to the truth. I needed one last burglary to convince Chief Sapling I wasn't the culprit."

Alice nodded. "Then, years later, Edna found the report my mom made, and she guessed Jenny was innocent. Only she wasn't sure who the culprit was."

Trudy said, "With time, she figured it out. She was an arrogant old woman. She sent me an invitation to the knitting circle, and I recognized the font—that fool had used the same typewriter to do the postcard. So I went to the knitting circle. She probably thought she could use it to get closer to me and discover the full truth. But I used it as a setup."

"A setup for murder," Alice said. "You knew from the burglary that Edna had a timer on the power, so you broke in and reset it. Edna herself told Hildegarde she had two break-ins—one was by Simone, the other was by you. Then, when the lights went out during our gathering, you got up, passed behind Hildegarde, and stabbed Edna. But how did you plan for Simone's presence at the window?"

"I didn't. My plan was to frame Jolene. Imagine my surprise when I learned Simone was in town and snooping around the Yarn Shoppe. You helped by making Captain Burlap suspect she was the killer. You handed Simone to me on a silver platter."

Now Alice understood why Cullen had been harassing Jolene. "You'd already broken into Jolene's home before the murder to plant evidence. An anonymous caller was going to point the cops in the right direction—and they'd find a sharpened knitting needle or two, suggesting Jolene killed Edna. But now the evidence could muddy the waters, so you needed Cullen to retrieve it."

Trudy frowned. "Stop talking. I know what you're trying to do: you're trying to distract me. But buying time won't help you. The cops are busy with Simone, and by the time anyone comes looking for you, Cullen will have buried your bodies in the woods."

"You have a lot of confidence in that guy," Alice said. "It must be nice to have a 'private investigator' working for you who doesn't ask too many questions or worry about what's morally right or wrong."

"He gets the job done."

"Look, Trudy, the game's up. Why don't you put down the gun and we can all walk out of here with no one getting hurt?"

Trudy chuckled. "How stupid do you think I am?"

131

Hildegarde made a sound like a long groan, muffled by the gag. She kicked and thrashed against her bonds.

"What's with her?" Trudy swung toward her, aiming the gun in her direction. "Stop that."

Ona nudged Alice. She nodded and lowered her eyes. Alice looked down, following her gaze. The drawer was still open, the sharp knitting needles heaped on top of each other. Alice glanced sideways at Ona. And gave her a nod.

Trudy took a step toward Hildegarde, who was kicking and flailing. The duct tape was coming loose. Trudy took another step toward her, reaching out to grab the fraying tape.

"No," she said, halting. She raised the gun and pointed it at Hildegarde. "Stop it!"

Ona reached into the drawer and grabbed a knitting needle. The clatter made Trudy look up. Her eyes widened.

Ona drew back her arm.

Trudy swung her gun back toward Ona.

The knitting needle whizzed through the air.

It struck Trudy's wrist, and she screamed.

The gun hit the floor.

Alice threw herself onto the carpeting and grabbed the weapon, while Trudy cursed and gripped her wrist, which was bleeding.

She turned her head and bellowed, "Cullen! Help me, Cullen!"

Then there was a crack and a slam from beyond Trudy's office as the front door burst open. A voice called out, "Police! Nobody move!"

Footsteps thundered, loud even on the soft carpeting, as state troopers poured through the reception area. They gathered in the doorway, guns raised and pointed at Trudy.

"Freeze!"

Alice herself had no intention of moving. She let out a long breath.

Turning to Ona, she smiled.

"It's over," she said.

"Another yarn wrapped up," Ona said, and winked.

CHAPTER 28

$\mathcal{A}$ week later, Alice was hosting an event at Wonderland Books—a knitting and books party. Books with knitting in them were on sale, including Ann Hood's *The Knitting Circle* and Clara Parkes' *The Yarn Whisperer*, and customers were encouraged to bring their own needles and yarn. For those who didn't have their own, a jar on the counter held knitting needles, and there were baskets of yarn placed on the floor.

Some customers browsed books, others knitted and chatted. Becca's diner provided coffee and muffins, and Mayor MacDonald, Lorraine, and Thor stood by the coffee urns, talking. Beau was chatting with Andrea from Bonsai & Pie, while Esther was flipping through the pages of *The Beach Street Knitting Society and Yarn Club* by Gil McNeil.

Over in a corner sat Lillian, Jolene, and Hildegarde, chatting idly while their knitting needles went click-clack. Hildegarde had recovered from her ordeal with Cullen and Trudy as if nothing had happened. She was the definition of stoic. When Alice mentioned how strong she must be, Hildegarde dismissed the idea with another Bible quote: "I can do all things through Christ which strengtheneth me."

Alice and Becca sat with their own knitting. Ona, relieved to have given up on the needles and yarn, worked on a piece of wood with a knife, whittling a figurine. It looked a lot like an ox. In fact, Ona was even giving it boots.

Alice enjoyed the peaceful work and, more than anything, the comfort of sitting between her best friends as the bookstore filled with cheerful chatter.

Someone spoke Alice's name. Glancing up from her knitting, she caught sight of Simone.

"I came to thank you," she said. "And to apologize. I—"

Alice put down her knitting and reached up, taking Simone's hands in hers. She said, "You came to a logical conclusion. No apology necessary."

"I jumped to that conclusion," Simone insisted. "And I'm sorry. I appreciate what you did to catch Trudy and bring her to justice for the murder and for the burglaries. Finally, my sister's name will be cleared. I also appreciate what your mom did. Knowing she was doing her best to help is a relief."

"It must be a relief to put this mystery to rest after all these years."

Simone nodded. "The truth can't undo the pain. It can't bring my sister back. But now I can take the first steps—baby steps—to move on."

Alice squeezed Simone's hands. "Trust yourself. You'll do great."

Simone squeezed Alice's hands back in a silent thank you.

"So," Alice said, "what's next?"

"Back to my performances. There's this legend in the industry—he's retired now—who's mostly known for his haunted house shows, but he started off in the circus. He's agreed to mentor me, so I can learn how to start a business of my own."

Alice laughed. "Dr. Fantasma?"

"You know him, huh?"

"He's a quirky guy."

Simone smiled. It was the first time Alice had seen a genuine smile on her face. She said, "Blithedale's full of quirky people, isn't it?"

"It's why we love it."

"Amen."

Alice watched Simone walk out of the bookstore. Another visitor caught her eye. It was Captain Burlap. She hadn't noticed him in his civilian clothes. He wore a flannel shirt and jeans and a baseball cap. As he came closer, he tipped his cap in greeting.

"Alice," he said.

"Captain Burlap."

"I'm off duty. I wish you'd call me Walter—or even Walt."

"All right," Alice said with a smile, "Walt."

Walt Burlap smiled, his dimples showing. He took her hand and shook it. "You did a fine job, detective."

Alice's ears grew warm and she couldn't hold back the grin.

Walt Burlap tipped his cap at her again, turned around, and walked out.

Becca nudged Alice. "That's high praise from a state police criminal investigator."

"High praise from anyone," Ona added.

"A little recognition isn't a bad thing," Becca said. "Which reminds me."

She pulled out a postcard from her pocket.

"Oh, no," Alice said. "Not again."

With a smile, Becca handed Alice the card. Then dug out another card from her pocket and handed it to Ona.

Alice held up the postcard, studying the front. It showed three images from Blithedale, one of the What the Dickens

Diner, the second of the Pemberley Inn, and the third of Wonderland Books.

"You made this?" Ona said.

Becca beamed. "Read the back."

Alice turned over the postcard. On the back was a printed quote:

"Kindred spirits are not so scarce as I used to think. It's splendid to find out there are so many of them in the world."
— L.M. Montgomery, *Anne of Green Gables*

Alice linked arms with Becca and then with Ona and pulled them close to her.

"My kindred spirits," she said.

* * *

Thank you so much for visiting Blithedale. Want a FREE short story ebook? Sign up for my newsletter updates on new books and I'll send the free story to you by email:

https://mpblackbooks.com/newsletter/

The next Alice book is coming soon!

MORE BY M.P. BLACK

A Wonderland Books Cozy Mystery Series

A Bookshop to Die For

A Theater to Die For

A Halloween to Die For

A Christmas to Die For

An Italian-American Cozy Mystery Series

The Soggy Cannoli Murder

Sambuca, Secrets, and Murder

Tastes Like Murder

Meatballs, Mafia, and Murder

Short stories

The Italian Cream Cake Murder

ABOUT THE AUTHOR

M.P. Black writes fun cozies with an emphasis on food, books, and travel—and, of course, a good old murder mystery.

Besides writing and publishing his own books, he helps others fulfill their author dreams too through courses and coaching.

M.P. Black has lived in many places, including Brooklyn, Vienna, and San Jose de Costa Rica. Today, he and his family live in Copenhagen, Denmark, where coziness ("hygge") is a national pastime.

Join M.P. Black's free newsletter for updates on books and special deals:

https://mpblackbooks.com/newsletter/

Printed in Great Britain
by Amazon

40667749R10088